A
Harlequin
Romance

OTHER

Harlequin Romances

by JANE CORRIE

1956—THE IMPOSSIBLE BOSS

RAINBOW FOR MEGAN

by

JANE CORRIE

Harlequin Books

TORONTO • LONDON • NEW YORK • AMSTERDAM • SYDNEY • WINNIPEG

Original hardcover edition published in 1976
by Mills & Boon Limited

ISBN 0-373-02020-1

Harlequin edition published November 1976

Printed in U.S.A.

CHAPTER ONE

MEGAN SHAW'S wide grey eyes were fixed sombrely on the girl seated opposite her. Iris Markway was, as usual, immaculately turned out; she must, thought Megan disparagingly, spend hours getting her war-paint on. Megan had never really liked Iris, four years her senior, and doubted whether she would ever have made a friend of her had she known her when they were both younger. Since Iris was a comparative newcomer to the small Wiltshire village Megan had been born in, the question was unlikely to be answered. When the reason for her visit was disclosed, Megan liked her even less.

Iris went on in her slightly affected drawling voice. 'Oh, Alain said it in a joking way, but I know he meant it, so for heaven's sake keep away from him and give him space to breathe.'

Megan's eyes sparked. 'Keep away from him?' she repeated indignantly. 'Well! Of all the . . .'

Iris got up leisurely and walked to the door. 'Well, someone had to tell you,' she said spitefully. 'I'm surprised you haven't taken the hint before now. If you must know, everybody thinks you're chasing him.'

Megan stood looking at the closed door, then blinked hard and slowly shook her head, making the brown unruly curls bounce. Iris had said he had asked her to have a word with her!

She sat down slowly. She wasn't chasing Alain. He had always seemed pleased to see her, had teased her as he always had. He couldn't think.... not after all these years. She'd looked on him as a brother—the brother she'd never had; anything else was simply ridiculous.

She thought back to last summer when he'd come home during the vacation, and recalled two occasions when he'd said he wasn't going to a particular social event and she had not attended either. Later she had found he had attended. Megan gulped and the tears began to swell in her eyes. She had only wanted to make sure he wasn't lonely. And all the time he'd thought... She brushed her eyes impatiently. What a fool she'd been! Alain lonely? Why, half the female population for miles around would jump at the chance of his company. Well, as far as she was concerned he was welcome to date the lot of them! Oh, she would keep away all right! To think she had been so pleased that he was coming home for good this time, all studies over, and the knowledge he had learnt put to practical use on his farm on the village outskirts. Just let him ask her how she was! Megan fumed. That was if she let him get near enough to ask!

She glanced at the clock, and with a determined expression went to the telephone. When connected, she asked Mr. Tilson the local grocer if the groceries were ready for Clock House. Megan had once done Mr. Tilson a favour by running them up to the farm, and had somehow got stuck with the job ever since. It was a natural request to make, as in the old days Megan had spent half her time on the farm. When she was told they were ready, she gave a small sigh of relief. Originally she had intended to take them up that afternoon; Alain wasn't due till one o'clock and she had hoped to see him. It was now almost twelve o'clock, so she would take them up now. That way she would avoid meeting him.

Slipping her cardigan on, she went to get the car, calling out to her father that she wouldn't be long. She doubted if he heard her, for as usual he was engrossed in his work, and not in this century at all but back in the sixteenth, searching out data for his latest book. With a guilty start Megan remembered that she had not typed his latest notes for him, and was at least three chapters behind. As she started up the car, she told herself grimly that there was plenty of time now. She was lucky, really, there was so much to do in her capacity as secretary to her father, and helping out with research, plus all his correspondence. She drove steadily on down through the village.

Mr. Tilson was talkative, and mentioned with

twinkling eyes how the place would soon become livelier. Megan knew he was only teasing her, but it hurt just the same. Did everybody in the village think she was chasing Alain? If they did, it appeared no one took it seriously except Iris. She banged the box of groceries in the boot of the car. 'Careful,' warned Mr. Tilson, 'there's some delicacies in there.'

Alain's housekeeper, Mrs. Smith, watched Megan deposit the box on the kitchen table. 'You're early,' she commented. 'He's not due till one. Are you staying on for lunch?'

Normally Megan would have asked if it would be a bother, and equally normally Mrs. Smith would have replied, 'No trouble.' This time she looked at the small grey-haired woman, who rarely smiled, but was not half so intimidating as she looked; Megan knew a kindly nature lurked behind her blunt remarks. It was odd, Megan mused, that after all this time, it had never occurred to her that people might think. . . . She shrugged these thoughts away. There was only Iris's word to go by, and Iris was definitely biased where Alain was concerned. She answered Mrs. Smith's question. 'Er . . . no, thanks, Mrs. Smith. I'm behind with Father's work and I must get up to date this weekend.' And that, she thought as she took her leave, would cover her for that weekend—if any remarks were made by Alain about her absence.

The surprised expression on Mrs. Smith's face did

not go unnoticed by Megan. 'You're not staying, then?' she asked, then added, 'Oh, well, you'll be up later, I expect.'

Megan's expression was grim as she started up the car. Mrs. Smith was in for a surprise, and so were a few other people if Iris was proved right. She was thankful that her father was too engrossed in his work to notice anything unusual—he would probably be grateful she had got down to catching up. She felt a rush of affection for him. Really, he was a dear, never upbraiding her for not keeping pace with him, only every now and again mildly enquiring how far she had got, and then only when he had promised to let the publishers have the book by a certain date. Megan would apply herself to the task, often working in the evenings to catch up, and had never let him down.

She turned off the lane leading to Clock House, and noticed idly that the wheat was looking fine—it should be a good harvest. Driving steadily on, she passed Hanks Meadow, and her thoughts went back in time. It was here that Alain had given her that first walloping. In spite of her depression she had to smile. She had been a holy terror in these days, and had been caught assisting the local poacher to land a salmon when Alain had come across them. The poacher, thoroughly experienced in these matters, had dropped everything—including the salmon—at the slight sound of a snapping twig in the surrounding shrubbery; leaving Megan wondering why her new-found friend had found it necessary to desert her in such a hurry. She was not long left in doubt!

Alain had been twenty-two then, and Megan fourteen. She hadn't spoken to him for days afterwards. Anyone else dishing out that treatment might have been forgiven by the tomboyish Megan, but Alain—her friend and confidant suddenly coming the heavy hand—was a bit too much to take. She frowned. Here she was, five years later, as mad with him now as she had been then.

In an odd way she felt betrayed. She had never got on with girls of her own age; her mother had died when she was five, and the memories had slowly faded with time. With a kind but absentminded author father, Megan had had a slightly bohemian upbringing. Mr. Shaw's sister had come to keep house for them for a time, then to everybody's surprise had married the Vicar. By then Megan was sixteen, and able to look after her father, and she had not taken too kindly to the strict discipline imposed by her aunt, who had been determined that Megan should receive adequate instruction on how a young lady should conduct herself. It had not been a successful venture. Most of the time seemed to have been spent on lecturing Megan on her mode of dress, which was anything that happened to be handy. When she was prevailed upon to wear a dress for a special occasion, instead of her beloved jeans, it would get torn, usually through climbing trees in answer to a challenge.

So Megan had grown up trailing after Alain, who was the only one who had treated her as a being in her own right, the only one she had been able to talk to, with her father in a world of his own, and an aunt who continually scolded her. She realised now how Alain had taken pity on her. She sighed. As Iris had cuttingly put it, she was a big girl now. She felt immensely sad. She had never envisaged a time when he would turn her away. It was like someone in your own family telling you to go away, that they no longer need you; and it hurt, it hurt very much.

She had just turned off the main road into the lane leading to the village, when she saw the car. There was no mistaking the bright red of his sports car. She knew he must have seen her, too, but she carried on as if she had not seen him. He had often accused her of daydreaming and said she was getting as bad as her father, particularly when they had an argument—he would think she was daydreaming now, she thought as she drove on through the village.

There was a lump in Megan's throat as she neared her home. There had been no hooting to bring her out of her daydream and make her realise he was home. He must have been relieved that she hadn't spotted him. Iris had been right; she hadn't really believed it, but what had just happened was confirmation enough.

Part of her understood. Alain was twenty-seven and would soon be starting to think about settling down. He was the last of his line and would naturally hope to have children. If he were courting, he would not want Megan around. Was it Iris? She shrugged. She could not see that as a successful association. Iris was a beauty, there was no denying that, but she lacked a sense of humour and took herself too seriously. Well, whoever it was, Megan thought crossly, she wished he'd get it over with and settle down; things then might start to get back to normal.

Letting herself into the house, she went through to the kitchen to prepare the midday meal. Only a snack was required as her father preferred to have the main meal of the day in the evening. Mrs. Jackson came in to do this; her aunt had arranged this when she had married, and the arrangement had never been altered. A morning help was also provided, a chore Megan could have taken on, but her father had thought she had enough to do in the secretarial line and argued that they could afford it.

As she watched the toast, it occurred to Megan that this argument no longer applied. The last manuscript had been rejected, accompanied by a long letter from the publishers regretting their decision not to accept his latest work. His previous book had not sold the required amount to make publication profitable, etc. The trouble now was finding a publisher who handled the type of work Mr. Shaw specialised in. As an historian he was hardly apt to produce a best-seller. There had been a steady sale of his work in the past, but things were getting tighter in the commercial world, as everywhere else, and the likelihood of finding another publisher was very slim indeed. The manuscript was now doing the rounds of likely firms, and Megan had got to the point of dreading the post these days, for all too often it would be returned.

She sighed as she buttered the toast. Everything seemed to happen at once. A few weeks before the publisher's letter arrived, another letter containing even more daunting news landed on Mr. Shaw's desk. A firm he had invested in heavily had crashed overnight and little could be salvaged. She had broached the subject of getting a job to help out, but her father had said there was plenty of time, they had had setbacks before.

Preparing her father's tray, Megan thought sadly of how she had planned to seek Alain's advice. Her father was no business man, and she recalled Alain's earlier doubts about this particular firm, now justified. She straightened her shoulders. Alain didn't want to know any more. She would have to tackle this on her own.

After lunch, she settled down in the guest room that he had converted into an office for her as the typing disturbed her father's concentration. As she typed away, she wondered if the history of the fells would fare any better than its predecessor, but very much doubted it. When she went downstairs to make a pot of tea at four o'clock, she heard voices coming from her father's study and paused as she went past. At first she thought it was Alain, and felt a surge of gladness, but as she listened to the different intonations she felt sharp disappointment. It was not Alain but someone she did not know. She moved on to the kitchen and proceeded to make the tea, adding an extra cup for the unknown visitor.

The man talking to her father rose when she entered the study. He was dark and well-built, tallish, and in his early thirties, Megan guessed. He was also very sure of himself, she noted, as he stood waiting for the introduction while she deposited the tray on the desk.

'This is my daughter,' Mr. Shaw said. 'Megan, we have another author in our midst. Ray Hallett, alias Vernon Hood.'

Megan held out her hand and smiled a welcome. She had heard of Vernon Hood, who hadn't? The most successful thriller writer of the day. 'Are you here incognito?' she enquired, thinking that there had been no gossip in the village. It would be a topic that would set the Women's Institute alight.

He smiled, showing even white teeth. Megan decided he was a bit too blasé for her liking, but he was extremely good-looking and would have no trouble, she thought, in attracting the opposite sex. At the thought of the unattached females in the village, between Alain and this charmer there ought to be some interesting times ahead. Megan wanted to giggle.

He answered her question. 'At the moment, yes, and I'd like to keep it that way. However, I have no doubt the news will filter out, especially when I refuse to join local affairs.' He grinned.

Accepting the tea Megan gave him, Mr. Shaw said, 'Well, you can ask her now. I've no objection, she's been threatening to get a job for weeks.'

Megan's brow raised as she asked whether Mr. Hallett took milk and sugar. He did, then explained, 'I'm seeking secretarial help. I heard about your father and came to ask his help in getting someone.'

Megan frowned. She didn't like being thrown at the man; for all she knew she might be entirely unsuitable. 'There are agencies in Salisbury,' she said, 'I'm sure they could find someone for you.'

Ray Hallett watched her with those knowing brown eyes of his. 'Don't you want the job?' he asked bluntly.

Flushing, Megan answered hurriedly, 'I only thought it fair to give you a chance to look round. You don't know if I'll be suitable or not, do you? And you might not like to tell me,' she added honestly.

'Works both ways,' he said smilingly. 'You may not take to my way of working. What do you say to a trial period for both of us?'

There was not much Megan could say to a proposition like that. It would have looked downright rude if she had refused. Whether she liked it or not, it appeared, she now had a job. A short discussion took place, and Megan was surprised at the hours he wanted her to put in—three in the morning, and two in the afternoon. The salary also shook her—she had never dreamt of earning that much a week.

'You'll find you earn it,' Ray Hallett warned her. 'I'm a bit of a slavedriver.'

It was arranged she should start work the following Monday. He had bought The Foxes, a house two miles out of the village, and that, Megan mused, would make him Alain's nearest neighbour. She couldn't help wondering what Alain would think of him and decided they wouldn't get on. She didn't know why she was so sure about this, but she was.

CHAPTER TWO

SUNDAY passed quietly for Megan and her father. It was decided between them that they would not mention their money worries to Alain. Megan knew her father was a proud man. 'He'll only offer to bail us out,' he commented.

For reasons of her own, Megan wholeheartedly agreed with this decision. Ray Hallett's offer had come as a windfall—a much-needed one. It would give them the breathing space they required until they had got over the hump. 'Mind you, Meg, if you don't like the job you say so,' advised her father. 'We'll get by. I've several publishers in mind.'

Planting a kiss on his bald pate, Megan said, 'I'm quite looking forward to it,' which was not quite truthful, as she was dreading the first few days.

Before she prepared for bed that evening, Megan sorted out clothes suitable for secretarial work. There was not much choice, for her wardrobe was on the slender side. Practically living in sweaters and slacks, her stock of dresses was woefully low, but at last she found a dress of light cotton material that would suit the purpose. She wondered if Ray Hallett would object to her wearing trousers, and did not see why he should.

Later, as she climbed into bed, she fervently hoped she would like the job and would be capable of holding it down. She also thought of Alain.

He hadn't even bothered to ring and find out where she was, let alone call in on them. Of course, he was always very busy the first week back, she told herself, he had so many things to catch up on. Still, she thought sadly, he might at least have rung.

The Foxes was a modern dwelling, and Megan, driving along its shrub-lined drive the following morning, trying to control the butterflies in her stomach, concentrated on the house in front of her. The previous owners who had had the house built, a retired bank manager and his wife, had never fitted in with the villagers. The man had been much too pompous and his wife of the opinion that money could buy anything. It was a help, Megan mused, but it hadn't bought them what they craved—bowing, scraping and servility from those they considered the yokels of the village. Finally they had given the villagers best and, after a few disparaging remarks on the unfriendliness of the locals, had left the district.

Getting out of the car, she wondered whether Ray Hallett would fare any better. On first showing she doubted it. He had an air of cocksureness about him that would be bound to arouse a certain amount of resentment from a few villagers she could think of.

Mr. Browne, for instance, on the District Council; a rather touchy character, but goodhearted when you got to know him. Of course, she mused as she walked to the door, Ray Hallett was a very successful man, and it must be very difficult not to let it go to your head. With his looks he was probably very successful in other ways, too. She wondered if he were married, although he had not mentioned a wife. Her thoughts were abruptly terminated at this point by the man himself answering the doorbell.

'Good morning, Miss Shaw,' he said jovially. 'Do you mind if I call you Megan?' he asked as he ushered her into the house. 'As we're going to work together, Miss Shaw is a bit formal, isn't it? Do come in, I'll show you to your den.'

Megan had no objection to his using her Christian name—everybody else did except Alain, who for some unknown reason of his own called her 'Tuppence'.

She followed him through the hall to a room at the end of a luxuriously carpeted corridor, then he opened the door and stood aside courteously for her to precede him into the room. She noticed that he was casually dressed, in a short-sleeved navy shirt and corduroy trousers. She thought she must remember to ask him if he objected to her wearing trousers, then realised suddenly that he wouldn't, and she didn't know why she had thought that he would.

The room she entered was a miniature office, a desk

complete with typewriter and dictating machine. Her eyes were riveted on the latter. She looked back at Ray Hallett. 'I usually copy Father's work from notes,' she said with a sinking feeling. She wouldn't be able to take the job after all, she thought miserably. Why hadn't she thought to ask? Most writers nowadays used tapes.

He smiled at her. 'Don't look so worried. It's not so difficult, you know. I might be a slavedriver, but I'm also human. I don't expect you to get through much while you're getting the hang of it. My last secretary took about a fortnight. I'm pretty certain you'll halve that time.'

Megan looked back at the machine doubtfully.

'Come on, I'll show you how it works,' he said cheerfully. 'The only real necessity with this work is knowing your spelling. Bad spellers are the ones who are really caught out. You'll see what I mean once you start.'

It did not take Megan long to learn the truth of this. She was able to adjust the speed of the dictation while she practised. His diction was extremely clear and very precise, so was his punctuation. By the Wednesday, she started to get to grips with the work, and the small pile of tapes waiting to be transcribed slowly dispersed. Nothing passed his attention—his office was next to hers, and she was instructed to just ring if she had any queries; it would be less tiring than running from office to office.

As the days went by, Megan found that she had badly misjudged Ray Hallett. She saw he was a kindly, thoughtful man completely engrossed in his work. Remembering his remarks about not being a sociable person, she wondered a little about this. She learnt he had a sister, who had come down from her home in the Midlands to see to the furnishings of the house and make sure her brother was comfortable before returning to her family after he had moved in. She had noticed a photograph of a lovely dark-haired woman on his desk and wondered if that was his sister.

The work she found utterly intriguing. She would avidly follow each chapter and try to work out the villain of the piece. Megan had not had much time for reading in the past, but she slowly became addicted to the detective story, and felt she would like to read Ray Hallett's previous books. At one stage of the story she was sure she had spotted the one vital clue to the killer's identity and told him so. He had smiled and asked her to name the character. She had done so, only to be told with a teasing twinkle in his eye that she had swallowed the red herring. Megan had accused him indignantly of deliberately misleading his public, and he had laughed delightedly. Then she had said curiously, 'I don't believe you know yourself until the last chapter,' which had sent him off into peals of laughter and he managed to get out: 'You know, Megan, you're perfectly right,' and left her wondering whether this really was so.

On Megan's recommendation a housekeeper had been found for him, and a daily help. Megan knew that Mrs. White in the village could do with the extra money and had given her name when her advice was sought.

It was on the Friday that a few of the questions Megan had pondered on were answered for her. She had asked if she could borrow a copy of one of Ray's books to read over the weekend and had chosen his first. Permission was readily given. 'I think I've come on a bit since then,' he commented with a smile.

Taking it from the shelf, Megan idly opened the book and the words, *To my loving wife*, leapt out at her. She closed the book hastily, feeling as if she had intruded on his personal life. Her abrupt action did not go unnoticed.

'Marie,' he said quietly. 'I lost her a few weeks before the book was accepted.'

Megan coloured. 'Please, Mr. Hallett, I don't want to pry. If you'd rather not talk about it . . .'

'I'd be grateful if you'd drop the Mr., Megan,' he said slowly. 'I think we know each other well enough by now for you to call me Ray.' He was silent for a few moments, then said quietly, 'No, I'd like to talk about her if I'm not boring you.'

Megan looked at him and instinctively knew that what he was going to tell her was going to be painful for him. Her soft heart was touched. 'Please, I'd like to hear about her,' she replied gently. 'And you're not boring me.'

He gave an odd, twisted smile. 'There are not many people I want to tell,' he said, and gave her a quick considering look. 'You know, Megan, there's a quietness about you and a refreshing frankness not many people possess—or if they did, life has knocked it out of them. I hope that doesn't happen to you. In some ways you remind me of Marie.' He turned away and picked up an old briar pipe and started filling it.

'In those days things weren't easy. I took odd jobs that gave me plenty of spare time to concentrate on my writing, and Marie kept on working—she had to, or we'd never have survived. My contribution was barely enough to buy the groceries, let alone pay the rent.' He paused while he applied a match to the pipe, then puffed for a second or two and continued. 'At first I was so sure I would be snapped up by the first publisher I approached. It was only a case of finishing the story and sitting back and waiting for the cheques to roll in....' He slowly shook his head. 'Well, I wasn't the first and I won't be the last to think that way.

'The first rejection somewhat brought me down to earth, the second and subsequently the third utterly demoralised me. Throughout this time Marie stood by, never complaining, always soothing and reminding me of the struggle other writers had in first getting their work accepted, and urging me not to give up. That first attempt never was accepted. I scrapped it and began another—only, I might add, after Marie's gentle bullying. Eventually the second one was accepted, but only after several more abortive approaches.'

He applied another match to the pipe, and after a few more puffs he went on, 'When it did come—success, I mean—it was too late.' He shrugged expressively. 'Oh, I'm not saying I wasn't heartened or untouched by it—just that it was too late to really mean anything to me. As I said, Marie was killed in a car crash. A dog on the loose cut across the road. She swerved to avoid it.'

Megan looked away quickly but said nothing.

After a second or so, he said, 'All that time, it was her faith in me I wanted to justify. To buy her the things she'd never had.' There was a wealth of bitterness in his voice. Then just as suddenly, the bitterness left him, and his voice now held a tired note.

'It took a long time to get adjusted and it was a long time before I wrote another book.' He looked back at the shelf from which Megan had selected the one she wanted. 'Ironically, despair brought out the writing talent. The next book was a best-seller. I never looked back after that. There were too many well-wishers, though—at least that was what they called themselves—I had another name for them. Always dropping in. . . . Oh, you know the sort of thing. Had I lost all overnight, they would have vanished into thin air.' He grimaced wryly. 'Marie and I always kept apart from others. We had each other and it was enough.' He sighed.

'After a few years, the matchmakers got to work. To my horror I found friends casually introducing single women or widows for my inspection.' He ran a hand over his hair and grinned. 'I think the married men envied my single state and tried to level the score, so like a coward I cut and ran, determined to get a bit and peace and quiet.' He looked at Megan. 'I envy your father, Megan. He's content with solitude, living as it were in the cool shade and out of the limelight. It's that shade I now seek, and with any luck I'll find it.' He gave Megan a conspiratorial look. 'You have my permission to dub me as an unsociable type, a misanthropist if you like. No doubt you'll be quizzed about me.'

Megan grinned back at him. 'An absolute slave-driver,' she said. 'And I wouldn't stay, only the money's good.'

He nodded approvingly. 'Excellent,' he smiled, 'I know I can rely on you. Now you'd better be off or your father really will believe the rumours. I hope you like the book, by the way, and have a good weekend.'

At the door, Megan hesitated. 'Ray,' she said doubtfully, 'what you said about Father—it was true, but he does appreciate company sometimes. I know he'd be pleased to see you if you felt like a chat some time.'

He smiled back at her. 'You're a very sweet girl, Megan. One day I'll probably take up your offer,' he promised.

That evening, Iris called on her. Megan was under no illusion as to why she had been so honoured. With Alain home, Iris was not the sort of person to bother about seeking out Megan's company.

It soon became clear that Iris was extremely put out. 'I know he's been away a year,' she complained, 'but he's been away just as long before and never made half as much fuss about the state of the property. He had poor old Mannings shaking in his shoes after he'd been through the accounts.' She threw back her long fair hair, a gesture Megan had often seen her make when annoyed.

Watching her, Megan's thoughts strayed back to last summer. It must be conceded, she thought, that Alain had paid Iris more than the usual amount of attention. All this Megan could see now, and she wished she had seen it sooner when she recalled how she had tagged on in their company. She had always considered Alain her special property and Iris an interloper. Inwardly sighing, she thought how often they must have wished her elsewhere.

Iris carried on, unaware of the thoughts racing through Megan's mind. 'Every farmer's taken a knocking these days, but Alain's sure he's taken more than his share.' She flung herself down in the most comfortable chair in the room. 'He's spent practically the whole week going over the estate with a notebook,' she continued pettishly, 'jotting down what needs to be done. I offered to go with him and make some notes for him, but he said he wasn't in the mood for any distractions.'

Megan almost chuckled. She could well imagine the scene. Alain's temper when roused was something to be respected; she doubted whether Iris had ever been on the receiving end before. No wonder she was put out!

'I expect he's worried, Iris,' she said. 'Farming nowadays is one big headache. He was very probably right in what he said about the losses. He's been at college studying the subject for two years, remember, so that the farm can be run more efficiently. It's not as if he's had no experience—farming's been in his family for generations.'

Iris pouted. 'Well, you'd think he'd have eased off a bit on his first week home. He has all the time in the world now to get things straight, no need at all to plunge into it with such fanaticism. Still,' with a note of satisfaction creeping into her voice, 'he did ask me to go to the county farmers' dance on Wednesday.' Then, as if it were something she had just remembered, she said, 'He asked where you were, and I told him you'd got a job. He said it was about time, you'd lazed around long enough.'

Megan's eyebrows lifted. 'Well, of all the . . . Just wait till I see him!' she said, quite forgetting her plan to stay out of his way.

'I thought we'd agreed you wouldn't hang around him,' drawled Iris. 'I shouldn't make an issue of it if I were you, he bit my head off for offering to help. I'd hate to think how you'd fare if you started trailing after him again.'

Megan's lips straightened. For one moment she was tempted to put a few facts at Iris's disposal. Firstly, and more important than anything else, she had a clear field as far as Alain was concerned. Their friendship was purely platonic, anything else was laughable. Not that Iris would see it that way, she thought sadly. It would be a waste of time trying to prove it to her. As far as Iris was concerned there was no such thing as a platonic friendship with the opposite sex. You either fell for them, or you didn't. She held her tongue.

'By the way,' said Iris casually, 'is it true that your employer's a famous author?'

Megan nodded warily.

'Young or old?' persisted Iris.

Megan grinned, for she could see the purpose behind the question. 'Oldish,' she said.

'Married?' queried Iris.

Still smiling, Megan thought Iris was running true to type. It was nice to be able to get some of her own back. 'There's nothing doing in that line,' she chuckled. 'He's not what you might call sociable, and a slavedriver to boot. Honestly, sometimes I wonder why I stick it.'

Iris's cold blue eyes rested calculatingly on her. 'Why do you, then?' she asked in a voice that said she didn't believe a word of it.

'The money, of course,' answered Megan promptly. 'The salary's fantastic. So I swallow my resentment.'

Iris got up to leave, her purpose now fulfilled. 'Well, we shall soon see how sociable he is, shan't we? I'm making a collection on behalf of the Church restoration fund.' She looked back at Megan. 'He's not an atheist, I trust?'

Megan grinned back at her, and asked a question of her own. 'How long have you been associated with that fund?'

Iris's eyebrows rose haughtily. 'Oh, I help out now

and again,' she returned coldly. 'What's the best time to call?'

Sadly eyeing her, Megan thought that she had no sense of humour. 'Would you like me to make an appointment for you?' she asked wickedly.

Iris stared at her. 'Is he that important?' she queried.

Megan nodded decisively. 'Oh yes. And he's a stickler for the proper procedure. Time is money to him.'

Iris was impressed. 'Er . . . well, perhaps you'd just mention I'm calling on Tuesday morning. What time does he have coffee?'

Ten out of ten for trying, thought Megan. 'Well, he has no set time for it,' she said carefully. 'I'll tell him you're calling, but don't blame me if he won't see you,' she added with relish.

That evening, Megan told her father about Ray. 'It just shows,' she said musingly, 'how you can get an entirely wrong impression of someone.' She looked at her father. 'Tell me, Father, what did you really think of him when he called?'

Mr. Shaw smiled. 'What he intended me to think, I'm afraid,' he said, 'a bit pompous.'

Megan's smile widened. 'It's a deliberate front he puts up to keep people away. Do you know what he said?' she asked suddenly, her head on one side. 'He envies you. He said something about your being content to live in the shade, or words to that effect.'

'Did he, now?' murmured Mr. Shaw. 'Well, he's right about one thing. I'm content.' He ruffled Megan's hair affectionately, then sighed. 'The manuscript was returned again this morning.'

Giving him a sympathetic look Megan asked, 'Want me to look out more names for you?'

He shook his head. 'I've still two in mind. I'll get you to post it off again on your way to work on Monday.'

CHAPTER THREE

MEGAN spent Saturday and Sunday catching up on her father's work. He protested, but she carried on in spite of his assertion that there was no rush now. 'I haven't anything else to do,' she said airily.

'Aren't you going to Clock House?' he asked. 'I thought you said Alain was home.'

'I expect Iris is there,' Megan said darkly. 'I don't want to cramp her style—or Alain's, come to that.'

Her father blinked rapidly and looked at her. 'Really, what odd expressions you use, child. What am I to deduce from that remark?'

Megan grinned impishly. 'Well, I'm not sure who's courting whom, but someone's courting someone, if you see what I mean.'

Mr. Shaw still looked slightly bewildered, then his brow cleared. 'Oh, Alain's courting, you mean? Well, it's about time he settled down, I suppose. Who did you say the girl was?'

She supplied the name again.

Her father frowned. 'Iris?' he said. 'Have I met her?'

Megan sighed. Her father rarely came down from

the clouds to meet anyone. 'The fair girl who called on Friday,' she said patiently.

'Oh, that one,' he said. He didn't sound awfully impressed, Megan thought. Iris would be pleased!

On Sunday evening Megan collected Chas, Mrs. Jones's dog. It had become a ritual for many weeks now. Mrs. Jones was afflicted with arthritis, and in the past had depended on a neighbour's help in giving the dog the exercise he needed. Mrs. Holm was not too sprightly herself and had willingly bowed out when Megan offered to help out. Chas was a very lively boxer, and had at first proved a bit of a handful for Megan's slight five foot two to cope with; however, after a few skirmishes, Megan had come out on top and Chas, with tongue lolling and eyes rolling, acceded her authority. They had now got to the stage when he came when she called him to heel, rushing up at a great rate of knots liable to test the strongest nerve. It had also taken Megan quite a while to get it into his head that the object was to come to heel, not to knock her flying.

As he rushed hither and thither, sniffing and snuffling in high delight at every new scent that presented itself, Megan walked ahead down the lane. She was quite proud of her prowess with him. She knew she had only to call, or indeed hide behind one of the huge old oak trees, and within minutes he would be frantically searching for her. She often talked to him on the way, such comments as, 'I don't know why Mrs. Jones keeps you. You couldn't guard a worn-out mat. You're an old softie if I ever saw one!'

On this particular evening, however, she was proved wrong. A voice hailed her from across the wooded section they had just passed. It was Alain. At first, Megan decided she would carry on as if she had not heard—she was still very annoyed with him—but she sighed, and then turned towards him.

He walked towards her, his long loping stride seemed to cover the ground twice as fast as anyone else she knew. He wore a thick navy blue polo-necked sweater and dark grey tapered slacks. His fair hair was worn in the current fashion but not too long, and Megan grudgingly had to admit it suited him. It reminded her of the medieval knights. Alain would have made a fine knight.

She pulled herself together. She was daydreaming again—as Alain had once said, she was beginning to live in the past as her father did.

Alain came one way and Chas the other. Chas reached her first and stood with curling lip in front of her, daring Alain to come closer.

'What the devil are you doing with that?' he demanded irritably. 'What's the matter with the brute?'

'His name is Chas,' said Megan, very much on her dignity. She could have hugged Chas. He was a watchdog, after all. 'I think he's guarding me,' she confessed, and found she was quite unable to keep up her haughty front. 'Isn't he clever? she grinned. 'Honestly, I've quite maligned him. I thought he was hopeless.'

Alain did not share her enthusiasm. He made an attempt to move closer, but Chas, having decided to adopt a protective pose, was playing it for all he was worth. A low growl broke forth.

'I'd have it muzzled if I were you,' Alain said. 'Haven't you got a lead for it?'

'Of course I have,' retorted Megan, and produced it from her jeans pocket. She clipped it on Chas, who threw her a half-startled, indignant look. 'Good boy,' she said. 'Friend, Chas. Come and make friends with him,' she invited Alain.

'No, thank you,' he replied caustically, 'I prefer to visit it behind bars, where it belongs. Who owns it, anyway?'

'Mrs. Jones,' Megan answered haughtily. 'If you remember, she suffers from arthritis, so someone has to walk him. And stop referring to him as "it". His name is Chas,' she added indignantly.

'So Chas it is,' he replied with some amusement. 'Come on, I'll see you both get safely back to the village.'

Megan bristled. 'We've not finished our walk,' she said crossly. 'You go on. I'll not let him off the lead until you're out of sight,' she added with a certain amount of relish in her voice. Alain was a great one for giving orders, but those days were past.

His grey eyes surveyed her with mixed exasperation and amusement. 'All grown up, are we?' he teased.

Megan flushed. He could so easily throw her off balance. She had never yet won a battle of words with him. You didn't argue with Alain, not unless you were prepared to take either a shaking or a walloping. She gritted her teeth. If she hadn't grown up now, she never would! 'I wish you would stop treating me as if I were still fourteen,' she said crossly. 'For your information, you're five years behind the times.'

'Doesn't time fly?' he enquired provokingly, with a wicked grin. 'However, you're still a plaguey menace to me, Tuppence.'

The use of his pet name for her did not help matters. Megan could only stand on her dignity. 'Well?' she said belligerently. 'Are you going? Mrs. Jones will be worried if we're not back by dark.'

His brows shot up at her determined attitude. 'She has every reason to be worried,' he said quietly. 'As for finishing your walk, not on my land you don't. I'm not having the brute flushing the chicks we've been rearing all winter.'

With a guilty start Megan had to admit the truth of this. On two previous occasions she had had to call him to heel when they had reached that particular section of the wood, where the pheasants were watched over ready for the start of the game season. Alain ran two shoots a year on a commercial basis. It was prohibitively expensive to take part, but nevertheless he was never short of guns. Business men came year after year, and in spite of the cost there was a waiting list. 'I keep him on the lead,' she said defensively, 'when we get to the hatchery.'

A rabbit shot out across the lane at that precise moment, and Chas had a lapse of memory where the guard dog part was concerned and shot after it, dragging Megan with him. After a short struggle and a good talking-to, Megan won the day. Slightly breathless, she looked up to find Alain still standing by with a sardonic expression on his face.

'I see I shall have to get Mrs. Jones to find someone who can control him,' he said, and took the lead from Megan.

It was too late for Chas to try and reinstate his position, and Alain's sharp, 'Down, sir!' took him quite by surprise, and he automatically obeyed. Megan thought he was a traitor.

'Might make something of him yet,' Alain commented. 'Not much more than a year old, I'd say. With proper training he could be a good dog.' He looked at the fuming Megan. 'Shall we go?' he queried, and went ahead anyway.

After a few minutes, he said, 'I hear you've got yourself a job.'

Megan, trailing after him, uttered a short, 'Yes.'

He looked back at her, and his eyes had that amused look again. 'You don't sound too enthusiastic about it. Your boss is a bit of a recluse, Iris tells me.'

The mention of Iris did not help, either. Megan's feelings were decidedly ruffled. 'Yes,' she repeated abruptly.

He sighed, and turned to face her. 'Come off your high horse and stop turning that apology for a nose up at me,' he said, grinning. 'Is it really as bad as all that?'

Megan surveyed him dispassionately. Once, she would have grinned back and launched into a narrative. Not now, she thought sadly. A few well-chosen words from Iris had ended a friendship she had valued all her life. Even if she had been tempted to tell him about Ray, she knew she couldn't. Whatever she told him now, he would later discuss with Iris; besides, she would be letting Ray down.

'The work's interesting,' she said quickly, and that, she told herself, was all he was going to get.

They came to the outskirts of the village and Alain stopped and looked at her. 'All right, let's have it. What's biting you? If you say nothing, I'll shake you until your teeth rattle. I haven't been away that long.'

Megan drew herself up to her full five foot two.

'Chas,' she said icily, 'may just take exception to that.'

He chuckled. 'If you think you can hide behind him for the rest of time, you'd better adopt him, then I'll really take him in hand. Now what's got into you? You might as well tell me now as later.'

Megan was a great one for the truth herself. He wouldn't like it, but he had asked for it. 'All right, Alain Drew,' she said, glaring at him. 'Did you or did you not hint to Iris Markway that you'd welcome a brief respite from my presence?'

To her fury he just chuckled. 'So that's what's biting you,' he grinned.

'Did you?' persisted Megan, determined not to be put off.

He pulled a wry face. 'Well,' he said, 'there are times, young Tuppence, when two's company, if you see what I mean.'

Megan's eyes sparked. 'Why couldn't you have said so, then?' she demanded. 'For goodness' sake, we know each other well enough, don't we? It doesn't matter a whit to me if you want to seduce all the village maidens. You only had to say you were courting and I'd have kept out of the way.'

He caught her arm roughly, and to her delight a low growl broke out from Chas. She glanced at Alain. He was absolutely furious, she had rarely seen him look quite so angry. 'Don't you dare speak like that again,' he said harshly. 'You always were outspoken, but by heaven, it appears I've been away too long. If I hear you make any more remarks like that, I'll give you the tanning of your life! You were right in one thing, though—what I do is no concern of yours. Just remember to keep that tongue of yours still if you've nothing more enlightening to talk about.'

Megan stood stunned. Whatever she had thought the result of the confrontation with him would be, it was not this. She had not meant to be spiteful or condemning, surely he must have known that? No one knew her as well as he did, not even her father. She gulped. He would know he had hurt her, but he hadn't cared. She stared at him, now striding in front of her with that determined walk of his. Once upon a time he would have laid an arm around her shoulders and apologised. Not now.

She swallowed convulsively. Iris had been right. 'What I do is no concern of yours,' floated back to her. She squared her shoulders and followed him back into the village. So be it.

The following evening Megan had her walk with Chas all mapped out. They would not touch Alain's land, but cut across the village to the recreation ground, once used by the local cricket team. It would not be such an interesting walk—no wooded scenery, but there would not be the risk of running into Alain.

He had changed beyond all measure, she told herself sadly. His sense of humour had completely deserted him. Was this what falling in love did to you? If so, she devoutly hoped it would never happen to her. She didn't know much about men in love, but she had once heard the village butcher trying to excuse his errand boy's shortcomings by explaining that the poor lad was in love. Perhaps she ought to feel sorry for Alain too; being in love didn't sound a particularly happy state of affairs.

This state of mind did not last long. Having got their walk organised, Megan was absolutely furious to find that Alain had had his threatened talk with Mrs. Jones, who proved most reluctant to let Megan walk Chas. 'Oh, dear, I felt so bad after Mr. Drew had spoken to me. It never occurred to me that he might have been a bit of a handful for you. You were so good in offering, I'm afraid I just took you up on it,' Mrs. Jones explained in her slightly fluttery way. 'He said he would ask the bailiff's son Sammy to take it on for me. Awfully good of him, I thought.'

Megan's lips straightened. 'I'm afraid Mr. Drew's got the wrong impression of Chas,' she said. 'He thinks he's vicious.' Mrs. Jones's eyes widened. Megan nodded. 'So you see why he doesn't think I can control him,' she grinned at the perplexed woman. 'Chas wouldn't let him approach me, you see, he stood on guard. I do wish you'd been there, I thought it was awfully clever of him.'

Mrs. Jones beamed. 'I knew he had it in him,' she said. 'Fancy that!' She patted Chas, who was standing beside her looking hopefully at Megan.

'Besides,' went on Megan, 'I doubt if Sammy would take him further than the pub. I can't see him tramping over the fields with Chas, can you? And I'm quite happy to do it, in fact I really enjoy our walks. He really is a pet. We'll keep out of Mr. Drew's way. To be honest I think he's just worried Chas will flush his birds, so I'm taking him across the recreation ground.'

Mrs. Jones looked relieved. 'I must say I wasn't too keen on Sammy taking over,' she confided. 'He's not what you might call dependable, is he? But as Mr. Drew had been so kind I more or less felt obliged to accept.' She collected Chas's lead and gave it to Megan. 'Now you're sure you don't mind, dear? I can find someone else, I expect. With Mr. Drew home I don't suppose you'll have all that much time on your hands,' she added coyly.

There was a glint in Megan's eyes as she clipped the lead on to Chas's collar. 'Mr. Drew being home won't make the slightest difference to my programme, Mrs. Jones,' she said grimly, and walked to the door.

The idea was born as she walked across the field. No wonder Alain had lost his sense of humour! She was in great danger of losing hers. Even little Mrs Jones, who was no gossip and more or less confined to her home, had assumed a romantic attachment between her and Alain. For heaven's sake, she thought wildly, how had it all begun?

She sighed. It was no use going back to the past. Now she could see Alain's point of view. It must be pretty embarrassing for him. She was in no doubt as to who had opened his eyes to the rumours; she was pretty certain that, like her, he had been in blissful ignorance of the village talk. Well, he'd done his best to scotch the rumours, she thought sadly, and all she could do to help was to keep away, as he'd more or less implied she should do.

If only she had Iris's looks, she thought miserably, recalling how the young men had flocked around her at the young farmers' dances in the winter. Megan had only gone to keep Iris company, but she needn't have bothered. She nearly always ended up talking to the older members of the community, or helping with the refreshments. She sighed again. There was no beau she could produce at the drop of a hat, proving once and for all she had no designs on Alain. No new devastating young man in the village she could cast sheep's eyes at . . .

She stopped suddenly in her tracks. But there was! Not young, but certainly devastating, she thought with a grin. Ray!

She thought of Iris's forthcoming visit in the hopes of meeting him, and her eyes narrowed. She was almost certain that Ray would find some excuse for not seeing her, probably leaving some money for the fund with Megan to give her. Her eyes sparked. If only she could get him to see her, Iris would do the rest! All Megan had to do was to look dreamy-eyed whenever Ray's name was mentioned. Iris was not slow on the uptake!

The more she thought of it, the more she liked the idea. No harm could come of it. She would join Ray's fan club with a bang! Her step lightened, and she called Chas to heel, making an extra fuss of him when he complied. She looked at his eyes as he lapped up the praise. 'I must cultivate that look of yours, Chas,' she told him gravely, 'I'll need it.'

CHAPTER FOUR

ON the Tuesday morning, Megan remembered with a guilty start that he had not mentioned Iris's visit. To be truthful she had not wanted to put Ray on his guard. He would answer the door and therefore have to meet her whether he wanted to or not. Her conscience won in the end, and she warned him of the impending visit, adding, 'If you like, I'll see her for you and say you're busy.'

There was something in her tone that alerted him. 'What's she like?' he asked curiously. 'Apart from the fact that you don't like her,' he added.

His intuition surprised Megan; she didn't realise she had been so obvious. In all fairness she had to admit grudgingly, 'Well, she's all right really. She takes herself too seriously, if you know what I mean—she's the village *femme fatale* and I think it's gone to her head.'

Ray burst out laughing. 'That's something that will never happen to you, Megan,' he said with amusement.

'I should hope not' she retorted quickly. 'Trouble is, she's no sense of humour.' She stared at the blank piece of paper she had just inserted in the typewriter. 'I can't see what Alain sees in her. Well,' she grinned, 'apart, that is, from her face and curves, I mean.'

'Alain?'

'Alain Drew,' she explained. 'Lives at Clock House. He's been away for a year, and has only just come back.' She frowned. 'Really Alain should have called on you first. He's the nearest thing the village has to the old days' country squire, and owns most of the land around here. Still,' she added, 'he's been busy catching up on chores around the estate.'

'And this Iris is his girl-friend, is she?' Ray queried.

Megan grinned again. 'Well, it's debatable,' she said. 'No one tells me anything these days, but from the way he's been acting it certainly looks like it.'

'And you're not too happy about it?' murmured Ray. 'Do I detect a certain touch of jealousy?' he teased her. 'I suppose he's young and good-looking?'

Megan looked astonished. 'Jealous?' she squeaked. 'Whatever gave you that idea? Alain's like a brother to me—or he was,' she added slowly. 'One of us has changed, and it's not me. He seems to have lost his sense of humour too. I expect that's what love does to you.'

He chuckled again. 'It's plain to see you've never suffered from that malady.'

Megan shuddered. 'No, thank goodness!' she said hastily.

'Nor even had a crush on someone?' asked Ray.

'No,' Megan said abruptly. 'But I know what you mean. The verger's son had one on me, and followed me about like a puppy-dog. I think he's given up now, he joined the Army last week.'

Ray's shoulders were shaking. 'Megan,' he said, 'you're as good as a tonic.'

A peal of the front-door bell reached through to them. Megan looked at Ray. 'That will be Iris,' she said. 'Do you want me to see her for you?'

Ray grinned back at her. 'Not after you've aroused my curiosity like that,' he said, and went to answer the summons.

'Don't forget to be very unsociable, will you?' Megan whispered across to him before he reached the office door. 'Or I'll never speak to you again.'

He chuckled and raised one hand as he left the office.

Ten minutes later Megan heard voices in the hall, and knew Iris was being shown out. She listened and could hear Iris's slightly girlish voice, only used when she wanted to impress someone.

A few seconds later, Ray joined her. 'Whew!' he sighed, passing a hand over his brow. 'I see what you mean. She is a bit overpowering, isn't she? Women like that frighten me to death. She tried to get me to attend a social function on Wednesday, county dance or something. I gather all the bigwigs will be attending, so she thought it would be nice for me to meet a few of them, but I got out from under. I coughed up for the Church fund and whisked her to the door. Next time,' he said firmly, 'we'll arrange something—a most important phone call or something that necessitates my immediate attention.'

Megan giggled. 'You weren't unsociable enough,' she said, 'or she wouldn't dare call again.'

Ray's eyebrows raised. 'It would take more than that to discourage that young lady,' he said. 'I've seen purposeful glints such as she had in her eye before now. I only hope you're right about Alain what's-his-name keeping her occupied.'

On her way home that evening, Megan encountered Iris. It was not an accidental meeting, Megan was sure.

'I've met your recluse,' Iris greeted her sarcastically. 'You forgot to mention that he was reasonably young and quite a dish, didn't you?' she demanded.

Megan gave her the sort of look one gives a spoilt child that doesn't know any better. 'Recluse was your word, not mine,' she said. 'I said unsociable, if you remember.'

'Well, I think he's the most attractive person I've ever met,' Iris stated grandly, 'much too nice to let hibernate. I suspect he's only marking his time until he finds suitable acquaintances. I shall ask Daddy to invite him to dinner one evening. I quite see his dilemma—a man in his position would have to be extremely cautious in choosing his friends.' She broke off and gave Megan a piercing look. 'You did lay it on a bit thick, didn't you? Hoping to keep him to yourself, were you?'

Megan seized her chance. 'Well, you can't blame me for trying. He's gorgeous, isn't he? I'm quite potty about him.' She sighed dramatically. 'Not that he'd ever look my way,' she added mournfully.

Iris's eyes narrowed. 'Well, at least you're being sensible about it,' she said coldly. 'Alain will be relieved. The trouble with you is that you're too obvious. You just lack experience, that's all.'

She left Megan all but gasping, but soon her sense of humour reasserted itself and she found herself grinning. She wondered what Ray would think when she told him that she was his number one fan. She frowned when she thought of Iris's remarks, and felt pretty certain she knew what she had in mind; two strings to her bow would provide spice to the chase. Perhaps with two other contestants it might have worked, but Alain was not a man to stand for any nonsense, and Ray, thank goodness, was way ahead of any schemes she might endeavour to embroil him in.

Her father was quieter than usual that evening, and Megan guessed he was starting to worry over the future. He had been waiting to hear from their solicitors and hoping the news would not be quite so gloomy as they had earlier intimated. She sighed. It looked as if he had heard and the news was bad. She wished she could wave a magic wand and have his book accepted this time. From time to time magazines would give him an assignment, but there had been no requests for quite a while; the old adage of *it never rains but it pours* was proving its worth in their case.

It occurred to her that it must be particularly galling for her father to have a successful author bridge the gap for them, an author whose work depended solely on ideas and did not entail the rigid research his work demanded. Not, she thought with loving fondness, that he would begrudge Ray his success, for success as such was not a thing he sought. He was content pottering in the medieval times, browsing through ancient manuscripts yellow with age. She couldn't, she mused, have chosen two more dissimilar authors to work for. She certainly could not complain of boredom.

The following morning while they drank their coffee, Ray asked after Megan's father and what he was working on at the present time. Her normally cheerful expression sobered. She told him, adding, 'His publishers refused the last book, you know. It's now doing the rounds; if it's returned again, there'll only be two left he can approach.'

Ray put his coffee cup down and glanced up at her quickly. 'Tried the American market?' he asked.

Megan shook her head. 'Do you think they'd be interested?' she asked doubtfully.

He smiled and walked over to one of the shelves and selected a book from it. He opened it, ran a finger down a list of names and gave it to Megan. 'The last three on that list,' he murmured. 'I'm pretty certain one of them will accept it.'

Megan stared at the names, then looked back at Ray, her eyes wide. 'Honestly?' she said.

He grinned at her. 'Well, try them and see. They rather go for that sort of thing in the States.'

Megan's eyes shone with gratitude. 'Ray, you're a brick!' she cried, then immediately sobered. 'Now there's only the problem of selling him on the idea.'

'Without telling him who suggested it?' he asked.

She nodded. 'He's awfully proud, Ray. I don't want him to think I've been confiding in you—which I have, but you know what I mean.'

'Well, why not just say I asked if he'd tried the American markets?' he grinned. 'It's not a lie. I did ask you, didn't I?'

With an eager nod, Megan had to agree. 'I'll sort of mention it in passing, then,' she grinned back.

The door bell went as she gathered up the cups, and Ray looked at her. 'If that's Miss Markham,' he said grimly, 'I shall definitely be unsociable this time.'

Megan soon identified his visitor. Alain's deep voice floated across to her. So he had decided to pay Ray a visit, then, had he? Had Iris bullied him into it? she wondered. Not that she could see anyone bullying Alain into anything, it was usually the other way around. She also wondered which attitude Ray would adopt, the unsociable or the pompous one. When she heard him ring for Mrs. Matthews, she guessed he was ordering coffee, and grinned to herself. It would be the pompous act. Alain would not be likely to repeat the call, or indeed hand out any invitation to the coming shoot, a thing he would most probably have done as an induction into the local society. Megan hoped things stayed that way. Iris would be disappointed, of course, but it was Alain who held the key of entrée to the village élite; if he approved all doors were open.

It occurred to her that his visit might be a case of sheer curiosity, a summing up, as it were, of Iris's judgment. She could imagine how Iris would have enthused about Ray. Yes, she mused, he would want to get a good look at someone who might turn out to be a rival for Iris's affections.

She was busily typing away when the door opened. Glancing up, she was surprised to see Ray, accompanied by Alain, walk into the office, 'Well, here she is,' Ray announced loudly. 'Slaving away as usual.'

Megan looked away quickly and hoped to be able to keep her face straight.

'I've come to ask your advice,' Ray went on. 'Do you think I ought to attend the County dance on Wednesday, Megan?' Before she could collect herself to answer, he continued in the slightly bored voice he adopted for these occasions. 'I always rely on my secretaries,' he confided to a poker-faced Alain. 'Especially if they're local.'

Megan was having trouble in suppressing her amusement. She dared not look at Ray. 'You'd hate it,' she said firmly, noting with pleasure Alain's lips thin.

'Yes,' murmured Ray. 'I rather thought I would.' He looked brightly at Alain. 'Well, that's settled, then,' he said airily, and began to walk to the door.

Alain stood his ground and looked at Megan. 'You are coming, of course,' he said, in a voice that dared her to say no.

Megan feigned surprise. 'No, I'm not,' she said hastily. 'I hate them too.'

Ray grinned. Alain looked from one to the other, his expression grim. 'Since when have you been a recluse?' he asked softly.

Megan coloured, but refused to give way. 'It's not a question of being a recluse,' she said coldly. 'Now I'm working I don't get quite so much time for socialising. I still work for my father, you know, and,' she added with a note of challenge in her voice, 'I walk Chas.'

'I thought I'd arranged for someone else to take that brute off your hands,' Alain said harshly.

'You did!' Megan replied tartly. 'But I talked Mrs. Jones out of giving the job to Sammy. Chas needs a good run each day, not a walk to the nearest pub.'

Alain's eyes warned her she had gone far enough. 'Then he'll get a good walk,' he said abruptly. 'By someone who can control him.'

Megan grew angry. 'We do not go near your land,' she said furiously. 'It's not my fault Chas took a dislike to you, and I look forward to our walks. I've got quite fond of him,' she declared dramatically.

Eyeing his stiff features, she realised with a spurt of surprise that this was the first time she had openly defied Alain and felt quite pleased with herself.

'Don't blame me if the brute turns on you one of these days,' he said between his teeth. 'I think I'll have a word with your father.'

'Father likes him too,' lied Megan.

Ray decided to intervene at this point. He looked at Megan. 'I'm not sure I shouldn't endorse Mr. Drew's warning,' he said. 'Are you really sure you can handle whatever it is?'

She shot him an indignant look. 'Of course I can!'

she said stoutly. 'He's really an old softie, you just have to get to know him.'

Ray wasn't convinced, and Alain's snort did not help matters. 'Then I think that's just what I'll do,' he said airily. 'I shall accompany you this evening, Megan,' he announced grandly. 'I've no wish to lose my efficient secretary.' He turned to the fuming Alain. 'Don't worry, Mr. Drew, I'll keep a strict eye on her.'

Megan could have hugged him. She now had a new champion, and if the glint in Alain's eye was anything to go by, he didn't like it one bit. Odd, really, he didn't want her around, yet he resented Ray's kindly intervention. He left shortly afterwards, giving Megan a curt nod to show her that he was extremely annoyed with her.

When Ray returned after showing him out, Megan met his amused eyes and asked half accusingly, 'Did you have to drag me into it? What would you have done if I'd said you ought to attend the wretched do?'

He grinned. 'Insisted on your presence too, to protect me.'

'And who,' asked Megan with raised brows, 'would protect me? I'd be swept under by the flood of local dignitaries wanting to make your acquaintance.'

'I rather think you can rely on your blond squire

to see to your welfare,' he teased her. 'Are you sure it's Iris he's courting?'

Megan threw him a look of disgust. 'You too!' she said exasperatedly. 'I did think you'd understand. The whole village, including Iris, is convinced I'm chasing him.' She sighed. 'Poor Alain, and poor me. We're just good friends—or we were, until last summer when he came home for vacation. He always seemed to be busy whenever I appeared on the scene.' She hit her small hand down on the desk. 'I didn't think anything of it at the time. He was always telling me to buzz off when I was younger,' her expression softened and she smiled. 'I used to follow him everywhere. A plaguey nuisance, he used to call me, but he was the only one who bothered to talk to me, *really* talk to me, I mean. Father was always wrapped up in the past, and when he did emerge he never treated me as a child but as an adult. You can imagine what a little know-all I must have seemed to the local kids, and what a lot of pampered ninnies I thought they were. You might say I was a misfit, and when I look back, I certainly was. They used to gang up on me and I was game to take them all on. It was always Alain who stood between me and annihilation. Not that I blame them, I was a holy terror!'

Her eyes twinkled. 'Mind you, he dished out some walloping of his own when I deserved it.' Then she frowned. 'How anyone could link us together in the romantic line is beyond my comprehension. We're more like brother and sister. He's years older than I am—at least eight.' She sighed again. 'No wonder he was upset when he heard the village gossip. So was I. Once upon a time we'd have had a good laugh about it,' she added sadly, 'now he's turned broody.'

Ray chuckled. 'So it's a platonic friendship, is it?'

Megan nodded vigorously. 'Exactly!' Her brow darkened again. 'Not that it will remain so if he still persists in trying to stop me taking Chas for walks. I know he's only trying to protect me in his way, but he can't have it both ways. If he wants to stop the village gossip he must confine his activities to looking after Iris's welfare. Oh,' she sighed impatiently, 'it's all so stupid, isn't it?'

Later that day, Megan hoped Ray would forget his promise to accompany her on her walk with Chas, but before she left he reminded her. She looked at him. 'Honestly, Ray, there's no need, you know. Alain's making a fuss about nothing. I'm sure you've more to do than walk the recreation field with us.'

'Nonsense,' he replied. 'A bit of exercise will do me good. Besides, I want to see this hound of the Baskervilles for myself. What time's off?'

Ray called for Megan at about seven. It had been agreed that it might be a good idea if he accompanied her when she collected Chas. 'You see,' Megan had explained, 'I think he only took exception to Alain because he suddenly appeared on the scene out of the blue, as it were. In his doggy way he wasn't sure whether he was friend or foe.'

Chas took to Ray and greeted him as an old friend just returned from foreign parts, particularly when he commandeered the lead. Mrs. Jones was thrilled when she heard the name of Megan's companion. It was quite clear that the news of his arrival had filtered through the village.

As they strolled across the recreation ground, Megan brought Ray up to date with local history of the village, while Chas went off on his excursions, every now and again racing back to join them as if to confirm that he was still with them.

'Well, I agree with you,' commented Ray as he watched Chas gallop up to join them once again, his four legs splayed out in what seemed an impossible physical feat. 'Your Chas is a big softie. I'm still trying to imagine him as a watchdog.'

Megan laughed. 'Well, I can assure you he was,' she gurgled. 'Alain was furious.'

They walked round the perimeter of the grounds until they came to the pavilion. Ray looked up at it. 'That's a bit ancient, isn't it?' he queried, gazing up at its weathered woodwork.

She followed his gaze. 'Well, it's been up about seventy years, I think,' she said. 'We used to have a fine cricket team according to the old residents. I'm afraid all we can manage now is a scratch team that turns out every bank holiday, and regularly gets a tanning. No one turns out to watch any more. It's sort of—demoralising.'

'Pity,' commented Ray. 'I always think a village ought to have a good cricket team. I say, do you think there's any chance of getting in for a look round? I've just got an idea for a story. I'd like to get the feel of the place.'

Megan was quite used to this sort of request. She had known her father once travel to Canterbury to re-visit the Cathedral when he was working on an article. Although he knew its history well, he still wanted to get, as Ray had just put it, 'the feel of it'.

'There used to be a way in round the back,' she said. 'Come on, let's see if the door is still left on the catch.'

To their delight it was. 'It must be years since I came,' said Megan as they entered the premises. 'We used to use the place as a headquarters when we were kids; when it rained, that was. I suppose the children still do. As long as no damage is done, Mrs. Sims turns a blind eye.'

They wandered through the musty rooms. Relics of past glories in the form of photographs hung on the walls of the changing rooms. Grinning moustached men holding aloft a huge cup, the date and names of the victorious teams faithfully recorded on plaques beneath the photographs. It was all so tidy and very dusty, there was a sense of expectancy, as if the place itself were waiting, waiting to echo once more the laughter and good wishes as each player strode out to do battle.

Ray sighed and murmured once more, 'Pity.' He sat down on one of the wooden benches that ran alongside the walls and went into a kind of reverie.

Megan, recognising the signs, knew he was reconstructing scenes in his mind. 'I'd better see what Chas is up to,' she remarked. 'He's probably going frantic trying to find us.'

A few minutes later she returned. Ray was busy making notes on an envelope. She waited until he had finished, then said, 'Did you pull the door to behind us, Ray? Because we're locked in.'

He pulled his attention back from his notes and looked at her. He frowned in thought. 'I believe I did. It was sort of swinging open, so I closed it.'

Megan sat down beside him. 'It's my fault,' she said. 'I should have warned you. The lock is dicey, one of the ancient types. That's why it's always left slightly ajar with a piece of cardboard jammed in. Mr. Simms the caretaker was always locking himself in until he had the bright idea of jamming the lock.' She grimaced. 'Chas is scratching like mad at the door. I made the mistake of talking to him. Someone's bound to guess what's happened and fetch Mr. Sims,' she concluded, but she didn't sound very hopeful.

Ray went towards the door. 'We'd better see if there's any other way out, hadn't we?'

'There isn't,' Megan answered mournfully. 'Not unless you're prepared to risk breaking a limb or two clambering down an old pipe from the scorers' den on the top floor, but I wouldn't advise it. It's coming away from the sides as it is. Any weight on it and it would collapse.'

'No windows elsewhere? What about the kitchen area?' he asked.

Megan shook her head. 'It's too tiny, even for me. Come and look.'

They looked, and Ray was forced to agree with Megan. They also looked at all the ground floor windows, not that there were many—just three, in fact—all boarded up.

By this time the light was failing. Soon it would be dark. Ray tried the electric light switch, but there was no joy. 'I suppose it's been disconnected,' Megan commented. Chas could be heard howling outside.

'Good old Chas,' said Ray with a grin. 'That ought to fetch 'em for miles.'

Megan was not so sure. The recreation ground was well away from the village proper. Someone else could, of course, be walking their dog, or even a courting couple might pass. She cheered up at this thought.

By nine o'clock, it was pitch dark. There had been a hunt for candles, which wouldn't have proved of much use had they found any, as they had no matches.

Megan, in cotton jumper and jeans, began to feel chilly, but said nothing. Ray, however, realised her plight and insisted on her wearing his sweater. It was more like a short coat on Megan and she was grateful for the warmth, but she worried about Ray missing the warmth himself. His thin silk shirt could not have held much heat.

He kept up a cheerful conversation on anything and everything. He knew Megan was worried about Chas, for one thing. 'Poor Mrs. Jones will wonder where we've got to,' she commented.

'How about your father?' asked Ray, as he settled himself full length on the bench.

'Fortunately, it's the evening Mr. Cane calls,' she said. 'They're old buddies and they settle down to a game of chess. It's more than I dare do to disturb them, so he won't even know I'm still out. Not till breakfast, anyway.'

She felt Ray look at her. 'Do you think I ought to make an honest woman of you, Megan, if we have to stay all night?' he asked in a teasing voice.

She burst out chuckling. 'You'll have the sympathy of the village if you do,' she retorted. 'They'll be certain I've lured you out here. I knew about that catch, didn't I? The fact that I didn't warn you absolutely smacks of intrigue. It is my fault, anyway. I ought to have remembered to tell you.'

'Well,' said Ray in the same light teasing voice, 'perhaps you did have an ulterior motive. You know if I were writing this up I'd make you a scheming wench. Your next step would be blackmail. Either marriage or cash.'

'Ray!' Megan sat up from her reclining position on the opposite bench. 'You don't really think I did it on purpose, do you?'

He chuckled. 'Of course not. But it would,' he said musingly, 'be nice to know you cared. I mean, it's a bit ego-dashing to hear you sound so horrified. I'm considered a good catch, you know.'

'Come off it!' retorted Megan, vastly relieved that he had only been teasing her. 'If I were really serious you'd be terrified. I've a good mind to start to act the vamp, although,' she grinned to herself, 'I wouldn't know how to start.'

He really laughed at this. 'You be careful, young Megan,' he warned her. 'For my part you're quite fascinating as you are.'

Megan did not have time to work out this intriguing remark, as a shout hailed them from outside. 'Tuppence? Where the devil are you? Have you got yourself locked in?'

Megan jumped up. 'Alain,' she said, 'Thank goodness,' and rushed to the door. 'We're in here, Alain! Can you get the key from Mr. Sims?'

'We?' queried Alain, a sharp note in his voice.

Ray spoke up. There was amusement in his voice. 'She's quite safe, Mr. Drew. It's my fault for closing the door behind us.'

'Did you have to say that?' hissed Megan. 'Now he's bound to think you're up to no good. Oh, dear!'

From the silence outside, Alain had gone to retrieve the key.

Ten minutes later they were standing outside the pavilion. Megan looked around for Chas. 'He's home,' Alain said curtly. 'I took him when I collected the key.'

'Oh,' said Megan. 'Did you hear him howling? He really is a clever dog, he wouldn't leave us.'

'It was just as well he didn't,' said Alain sourly. 'I called on Mrs. Jones and she told me you weren't back.' He looked hard at Ray. 'What were you doing in the pavilion anyway?'

Ray spoke casually, but Megan sensed he did not like the way the question had been asked. 'My fault entirely,' he said mildly. 'I wanted to see the inside.'

'Did you now?' said Alain, a wealth of meaning in his voice.

Megan started. Alain's stance looked forbidding; he was spoiling for a fight. 'And I stupidly didn't remind him to leave the door on the catch,' she said quickly. She then attempted to bring a light note into the strained atmosphere. 'It's all right, Alain,' she said airily, 'Ray did offer to make an honest woman of me if we had to stay the night.'

Instead of helping, it appeared to make things worse. 'It's as well I called on Mrs. Jones, then, isn't it?' Alain said through clenched teeth. He looked at Ray. 'Megan,' he said quietly, 'is apt to let her tongue run away with her. I can only advise you not to take her seriously.'

Megan gasped and glared at Alain. 'In other words I'm a liar, am I?' she ground out.

Ray answered smoothly, but Megan knew he was grinning. 'I can assure you I have our Megan weighed up,' he said infuriatingly, 'and I'm much too fond of her to take advantage of her, if that's what you had in mind,' he added quietly, then turned to her. 'Come on, I'll see you home.'

Alain barred the way. 'Thank you, Mr. Hallett, I'll see Megan back. I want a word with her father.'

To Megan's sensitive ears, this sounded ominous. 'Father's got company,' she said quickly. 'Ray's going my way and I'm not in the mood for a lecture,' she added belligerently.

'In that case, we'll both see you home,' said Alain determinedly.

One on either side of her, they started off. Megan

felt awful, like a small girl who had been caught out in some dreadful misdemeanour, now being marched to the headmistress's office by the prefect. It was an uncomfortable journey. Ray had tried once or twice to introduce a casual topic of conversation, mostly addressed to Megan and once to Alain, the result being an offhand answer bordering on a deliberate snub.

Megan marvelled at Ray's patience, and had a feeling that he was only biding his time until she was out of earshot before giving Alain a piece of his mind. She wished fervently she could be present. It would make a nice change for Alain to be on the receiving end. To think she had longed for him to be home again! She had forgotten the way he used to treat her as a small child, and the way he used to order her around. She had got used to her independence, and here he was trying to take up where he had left off. Well, she wasn't going to let him! It would be a good thing when he married Iris, she thought crossly. Iris would not let him spend his time harassing her; she wasn't one to take a back seat.

When they reached Megan's home, Alain did not carry out his threat of seeing her father. He might, of course, have changed his mind after she told him he had a visitor—on the other hand, Megan had a feeling he had sensed Ray's determination to have things out. Knowing Alain, Megan was sure he would welcome such a confrontation with relish. She devoutly hoped it would not come to a fight between them, for she was very fond of both of them and it was all so ridiculous.

She resisted the temptation to stand back a little way in the hall after the door had closed on her. If they had it out there and then, she could have heard what was said, but Megan was no eavesdropper and she went to her room after calling goodnight to her father, for which she received an absentminded grunt in response.

Usually she fell asleep as soon as her head touched the pillow, but not that night. A note of dissension had entered her hitherto peaceful existence. She had predicted Alain's reaction to Ray, but she had not foreseen the outright, barely concealed hostility he had shown that evening.

CHAPTER FIVE

THE following morning when Ray entered her office, Megan glanced up at him anxiously. She could see no signs of a fight. She almost gave a sigh of relief as her gave her his usual cheery, 'Good morning, Megan.' She longed to know what the result of the confrontation had been, but couldn't very well ask.

After a few desultory remarks, Ray brought up the subject himself. 'I have a feeling Sir Galahad will try and persuade you to leave,' he said with a grin.

Megan's brows raised and she shot him a look of comic exasperation. 'I'm way ahead of you,' she replied. 'Knowing Alain, I guessed that would be his move. Was it very bad last night? He went for you afterwards, didn't he?'

His smile widened. 'He didn't exactly have things all his own way,' he said. 'He was extremely vocal. I won't bore you with the details, but I was, as you might say, well and truly warned off.'

Megan's eyes sparkled. 'Isn't he the pink limit!' she exclaimed.

Ray's expression sobered for a moment. 'You know, in his position I'd have done the same thing.'

Megan stared at him.

'Look at it this way,' he explained. 'He doesn't know me from Adam. I could be a second Bluebeard; being a success doesn't automatically make me a pillar of society, does it? In some cases it works out quite the opposite. Then he has this thing about you.'

Megan interrupted quickly. 'Only because he still thinks of me as his kid sister,' she assured him.

He gave her a considering look, then continued. 'Well, as I was saying, in his shoes I'd have done the same thing. In fact I would most probably have knocked the fellow down, and he almost did. I could see he was itching to plant me one. However, I managed to keep my temper and swallow the extremely cutting remarks calculated to make me take a swing at him.' He smiled. 'I'm sure he's now convinced I'm a coward as well as a lady-killer!'

Megan looked contrite. 'It must have been hateful for you. I know Alain when he gets on his high horse. He didn't give you a chance, did he?'

'I don't think he's anything against me personally,' Ray replied. 'Any male would have come within fire in those circumstances.' He shot her a quick, bemused look. 'Can I take it you will stand by me?' he asked, half seriously.

Megan looked surprised at the question. 'Of course!' she said indignantly, then grinned. 'Besides, I need the money, remember?'

Later, as she sat typing, Ray's words came back to her; not only what he had said but what he had implied. He really did think there was more to Alain's protective attitude towards her. She sighed. Like Iris, he didn't know the background, although she thought she had explained that to him. Iris. . . . Her eyes widened. Of course! It explained the whole thing! Alain's aggressive approach . . . everything. Her lips straightened. Iris must have laid it on with a trowel! She did it purposely, Megan thought, just to make Alain jealous, and it had worked. It wasn't Megan he was warning Ray off, but Iris, using Megan as an excuse to have a go at Ray.

In a way she felt sorry for Alain, and was absolutely furious with Iris. Alain was too nice a person to be put through those kind of hoops. She was a little sad too, for she had not thought Alain would fall for such obvious tactics, and she sighed. That was love. The most rational of men were apt to behave in a most irrational way.

When Megan reached home that day, she found her father pottering in the garden. She frowned, for that was a sure sign he was worried. The garden, such as it was, was mostly lawn and shrubs, the easiest arrangement for a busy man with little interest in the horticultural line. As she walked towards him she rehearsed in her mind how she would bring up the subject of the U.S. publishers.

He glanced up from his perusal of a rhododendron bush. 'Ah, you're back,' he said, then turned and looked towards the house. 'It's a bit big for us, you know,' he mused. 'Ought to put it on the market and look for a smaller place.'

Megan gulped. She realised he was only facing facts. What he really meant was that he couldn't afford the upkeep of the house much longer. Considering how much he loved the place, it must have been a painful decision for him; she chided herself for not mentioning Ray's suggestion, although there had not been a suitable occasion before now.

In the event it was easier than she had imagined. She casually mentioned her conversation with Ray, after her father had informed her of the returned manuscript. He had glanced up at the innocent-looking Megan and muttered, 'I wonder?'

Megan would have loved to have produced the names Ray had given her, but it would have looked too obvious. Mr. Shaw looked back at her. 'You might ask him if he's any particular firm in mind,' he said slowly.

Megan threw caution to the winds. 'He has,' she said quickly, and giving him a wicked grin produced the names.

'That was quick work,' he commented dryly.

Megan chuckled, and gave him a quick hug. 'He's

absolutely certain the first one will be interested. You will send it, won't you?' she pleaded.

'I suppose I shall have to,' he said musingly, 'considering the trouble you two have gone to.'

Collecting Chas later for his walk, Megan felt as if a weight had been taken off her shoulders. She somehow knew that everything was going to work out fine. Her father would place the book. She felt a rush of gratitude towards Ray, and blessed the day he came to the village. Even the previous day's incident did not mar her thoughts. It would not take long for Alain to see that Ray had absolutely no interest in his Iris, and the whole thing would just blow over. In fact, it was highly probable that they would become firm friends.

Mrs. Jones was talkative. She was full of the previous evening's happenings. 'Dear Chas,' she said. 'Mr. Drew told me what happened when he brought him back. Just think, if Chas hadn't stopped with you you'd have had to spend the night in that place! I do think it's about time Mr. Sims did something about that lock, you know.' She carried on quickly, 'I was beginning to be worried, you know, and I did wonder whether you'd gone back to The Foxes with Mr. Hallett. Is he really Vernon Hood?' she broke off to ask suddenly.

Megan nodded. There was no point in denying the fact.

'Oh, isn't it exciting!' exclaimed Mrs. Jones. 'Why, only a few months ago they did a serial on TV of one of his stories, *The Golden Glove.* Just fancy that! Our little village will soon be in the limelight, won't it?'

'I do hope not,' Megan said hastily. 'Mr. Hallett came here for peace and quiet, you know.'

Mrs. Jones nodded understandingly, then said with a note of satisfaction in her voice, 'To think that I actually met him! I've read all his books!'

Megan's happy mood continued as she walked Chas across the recreation field. It did not even disperse when she caught sight of Alain striding towards her. She guessed his mission, but felt confident of allaying his suspicions of Ray's character.

For a while he walked beside her and talked of the estate matters. Although suspecting she was just being lulled into a false sense of security, Megan listened with interest, because she *was* interested. She had grown up roaming about the estate, tagging along behind Alain. She understood the problems entailed in running it, apart, that was, from the farm area.

When he suddenly changed the subject, she was ready for it.

'Tuppence, I don't think you ought to continue working for that man,' he said abruptly.

Megan feigned surprise. 'Ray, you mean?'

He shot her a quick look of warning. The trouble was, thought Megan, he knew her too well.

'Christian names with employers, especially employers you don't know very well, is to my way of thinking impertinent. Doesn't he object?'

Megan refused to take exception to that. If Ray could keep his temper, so could she. 'As if I would use his Christian name if he hadn't requested me to do so,' she said patiently.

'I suppose it makes him feel popular,' murmured Alain disparagingly, then snorted, 'A writer!'

'My father is a writer,' said Megan, finding it hard to keep a rein on her feelings.

'Authentic,' snapped Alain, 'not fictional.'

'Both,' ground out Megan, 'give pleasure in their own way.'

Alain did not answer for a few seconds, then he suddenly barked out at her, 'Was he telling the truth last night?'

Megan gasped. She stood still and glared at him. 'What's got into you?' she demanded. 'Of course he was. For goodness' sake! What would a man like that see in me? I'm as safe with him as I am with you or Father.' It occurred to her quite suddenly that he was genuinely worried about her. 'He'd have to be jolly well hard up to make a pass at me, wouldn't he? Not that I'd recognise one if he did.' She grinned at him. 'Remember me? The plaguey pest?'

Alain stood looking at her. With slightly narrowed eyes he took in her slight, boyish form, her hands on her hips and feet slightly apart. Her wide grey eyes humorously watching him, her curly head on one side.

'Congratulations,' he said quietly. 'You've grown up.'

Megan laughed delightedly. 'I told you so, didn't I? But I'm still the same. I haven't changed.'

'Haven't you?' he murmured, and his eyes swept slowly over her again.

'Stop looking at me as if I were some farm animal you were thinking of putting an offer in for!' she said indignantly.

His brows rose. 'Nothing was further from my mind,' he said softly. 'I do wish you would watch your words. Can't you see how a man like Hallett would take a speech like that?'

Megan did not answer; she was thinking sadly of how Alain had lost his sense of humour. She was positive he would have seen the funny side of the whole thing by now.

Alain continued, 'Not that he'll try anything now, he got the message last night.'

Megan was too sad to argue the point any longer. She was still a little girl where Alain was concerned, in spite of what he'd just said. 'No, Alain,' she said submissively.

He gave a quick piercing stare, not sure if she were

really meek or playing him up. Her eyes gave him the answer. 'Tuppence?' he said. There was a note of surprise in his voice. 'You haven't got a crush on him, have you?'

Megan sighed. Of course, it would have to be an adolescent thing like a crush, wouldn't it? He wouldn't register the fact that she might have fallen in love. It also occurred to her that Iris had not passed on the message, in spite of her assertion that Alain would be relieved that she had turned her sights elsewhere. She was back to square one, she thought. She sighed dramatically. 'I think he's wonderful,' she said, and sighed again for good measure.

He stared at her, his lips thinned. 'That settles it,' he said firmly. 'You leave this weekend. Do you hear? No—you'll leave straight away.' He sounded exasperated. 'I'm going to have a word with that father of yours. It's time he came down from the clouds and looked after you. Why on earth he didn't marry again and provide you with someone to look after your welfare I'll never know. You're fair game for a man of Hallett's stamp.'

Megan came out of her miserable musings. He wasn't even being brotherly now, but treating her as a nuisance he could have done without. Clearly he felt responsible for her. 'You'll do no such thing!' she rounded on him furiously. 'Leave me alone, Alain Drew! I don't need your lectures or interference.

Between you and Iris I've just about had enough. For goodness' sake look after your own affairs and leave me alone!'

His eyes widened at her vehemence. 'And what has Iris been up to?' he asked mildly.

Megan flushed and looked away, wishing she had held her tongue. It was too late now. 'If you must know,' she said between clenched teeth, 'she thinks . . .' she swallowed, 'she thinks I've got a thing about you.'

He threw back his head and laughed in pure enjoyment. Megan eyed him dispassionately. 'Go on,' she said, goaded beyond any reason. 'Have a good laugh. It is funny, isn't it? As if you and I could ever be linked that way.' As quickly as it had come, her fury left her and she started chuckling too. 'It's an absolute howler, isn't it?' she managed to get out. 'Just imagining it's a mind-boggling proposition. I didn't think even Iris could have been that stupid.'

He sobered for a moment and cast her a look of comic hurt. 'Thank you for those kind words,' he said dryly. 'I now withdraw my suit. I shall follow my predecessor and join the Army.'

Megan blinked back the tears the laughter had brought to the surface. She didn't know Alain had known about John. 'You know,' she said, the laughter still lingering in her voice, 'you sound just like Ray.'

He gave her a sudden hard look, the amusement gone. 'We do seem to have wandered off the point, don't we?' he demanded. 'I suppose it's no use asking you to leave?'

Megan shook her head decisively. 'I need the money,' she murmured with twinkling eyes.

'I'm sure you do,' he said sardonically. 'Since when have you yearned for the gold stakes?'

Again Megan regretted her words. It was not easy fooling Alain, she was not used to having to watch her every word. She took refuge in gaiety. 'Well, a girl never knows, does she? I mean, bottom drawer and all that bosh,' she said lightly.

He stared at her. 'You're not seriously considering Hallett?' he demanded. 'He's years older than you are. Haven't you wondered why he suddenly bolted here? He says he wants peace and quiet, but I'm not sure there's not more to it.' His voice grew gentle. 'Watch your step, Tuppence. In all probability he's married, and I wouldn't want you to get hurt.'

Although Megan knew he was concerned about her, she still felt it unfair that Ray should have been condemned out of hand. 'You know nothing about him,' she said quietly. 'And I think it's unkind of you to pass judgment like that. You didn't even give him the benefit of the doubt last night, did you? What would you say if I told you I'd engineered the whole thing?'

Again she noted his eyes widen in sudden surprise,

then they narrowed. 'If you did,' he said harshly, 'then you ought to be whipped. I'm only sorry I came on the scene. You would have received the shock of your life. That type doesn't play around. You'd be a new experience for him, but don't expect me to pick up the pieces when your dream bubble bursts in your face. You're a little green girl, nowhere near his mettle. Go ahead and burn your fingers—you've got to learn some time, I suppose. Thank heaven I can now wash my hands of you! You've refused to take my advice and that's good enough for me.'

He strode off, leaving Megan staring after him. She had rarely seen him quite so put out. At least one thing had been accomplished, he would not interfere in her affairs again. He was a man of his word. Megan knew he had now left it up to her. Either she did as he wished or the friendship was over.

She caught her bottom lip to stop it trembling. She couldn't leave even if she wanted to, and she didn't want to; she was happy, apart from the much-needed cash angle.

She called Chas to heel and began the return journey. The happy mood she'd started out in had fled, leaving a miserably hollow feeling. Things would never be the same again. She was as positive about that as she had been about her father's affairs straightening out for the better.

Her eyes were bright with unshed tears. She had lost her big brother, and a warm comfortable feeling that he was always there in the background. She had to admit sadly that it was for the best. It had to happen some time—when he married, for instance—she might as well get used to it now as later.

CHAPTER SIX

TWO weeks passed. Megan had no time to mope over her last meeting with Alain. True to his word, he had not attempted to seek her out. On several occasions while she walked Chas in the evening, she found herself hoping he would put in an appearance, yet she knew he would not. Ray had accompanied her on one or two occasions, and Megan knew the village was speculating on this new development and avidly watching points. She studiously avoided any get-together organised by the village's various committees, particularly if she knew Alain would be attending. She found she was much sought after to attend such functions and knew it was hoped Ray would accompany her.

Soon it would be harvest time, and the thought made her sad. It had always been a big occasion in the village—first the church service for the thanksgiving, then the harvest supper held at Clock House. Megan had always had a lot to do with these arrangements. Baskets of fruit and vegetables were made up, not only for the estate employees, but for the older folk of the village, a custom carried down from the ages by Alain's family. One had to make certain that no one was left out, and this had been Megan's task. Iris would now take it on, she thought, and hoped she wouldn't act the Lady Bountiful when taking them round to the older folk, or there would be some sharp reactions.

On the Monday of the third week, a cablegram was received from the American publishers. The book had been accepted, contract to follow. Mr. Shaw handed it to Megan as soon as she walked in that evening, and she gave a whoop of joy. 'I knew it!' she cried. 'Ray said they would!'

After dinner Megan hastily cleared away and washed the dishes. When this was done, she called, 'I won't be long,' and got the car out, and headed for The Foxes. She couldn't wait until morning to tell Ray the good news and thank him.

When she got there she decided she would not use the key he had given her to let herself in in the mornings. He was not expecting her to call and she felt it would be presumptuous of her just to walk in. She rang the bell.

'Why didn't you use the key?' asked Ray on seeing her. 'Come on in. I've . . .'

Megan didn't let him finish. 'I'm not staying,' she said hastily. 'I just wanted to tell you Father's heard from the American firm, and they've accepted the book!' Her eyes shone. 'Oh, Ray, I could kiss you!'

she cried.

His eyes twinkled. 'What's stopping you, then?' he said teasingly.

Megan grinned, 'You asked for it!' and reached up and kissed him on the cheek. Ray's arms came round her and he gave her a slight hug.

Drawing back from the embrace, Megan stiffened as she caught sight of someone standing behind Ray in the hall. It was Alain. She felt her cheeks burn and wished she could sink through the floor. 'I must get going,' she said hastily. 'I haven't taken Chas out yet.'

The gears grated as she swept out of the drive. She could still see Ray's wicked grin and Alain's cold eyes. Heaven knew what he had thought of that little episode, she thought bitterly. What was he doing there anyway? Ray's mention of a key made her cheeks start to burn again. Alain wouldn't have missed that, she thought.

She had never ever called on Ray in the evening. When he accompanied her on her walk with Chas, he always collected her from her home, and the one evening she chose to visit him, Alain had to be there! Why hadn't she seen his car? She would at least have had some warning, and shot off home again. Then she realised he would have entered the back of The Foxes, cutting the journey by going through the estate.

Well, it was done now, she thought wearily. She

wouldn't have had a thing like that happen for the worlds. So Alain had been unreasonable, but at least he had thought enough of her to try and save her from herself, or so he thought. In her headlong rush to thank Ray she had unwittingly destroyed any hope of ever getting back to the familiar pattern of the past. He would not only be angry with her, but utterly disgusted as well.

As she let herself into the house much later that evening, after taking Chas out, her eye caught a slip of paper on the hall floor where it had landed through the letter-box. Picking it up, she frowned. There was no need to read beyond the first few words, she was well acquainted with this type of missive, in fact she had typed them out before now at previous harvest times. It was a general invitation to the harvest service and supper, slipped in letter-boxes so that no one felt excluded. Megan had usually done the rounds herself.

Her brow creased again. Who was doing it now? Whoever it was must be new to the village if they had bothered to deliver it here. Her presence was taken for granted. She shrugged, and crushed the slip up into a small ball and placed it in the waste bin.

Emerging from the study, her father asked, 'Did you see Alain?'

Megan started. 'Did he call?' she asked, feeling a

tiny hope spring up.

'No, he didn't,' answered her father. 'I must say I was a bit disappointed. I happened to glance out of the window when I heard the car. When he didn't come in but left almost immediately, I assumed he was looking for you.'

She answered lightly enough, in spite of her feelings. 'I suppose we missed each other,' she said casually. 'What with me working, and his affairs to catch up on, we don't see much of each other now.' She hoped this sounded plausible.

Mr. Shaw grunted. 'Even so,' he complained, 'he might have looked in, mightn't he?' and he went back into the study.

Megan went to her room. She was extremely depressed. There was only one person who could have delivered that invitation. Alain.

She gazed out of the window towards a clump of pines in the distance, the start of Alain's land. Slowly the sadness faded and a glint appeared in her eye. Of all the rotten things to do! Treating her as a complete stranger! For that was what those slips were for. People new to the village, or others who did not usually participate in local affairs. Considering the amount of help she usually gave at that function, it amounted to a direct snub. It was his way of saying, you are welcome to come but don't expect any preferential treatment. It was also a way of saying her help would not be required that year. Which was just as well, she fumed, because she didn't intend to give any!

She shook her head. What on earth had got into him? This was not the Alain she had once known. Iris was probably giving him a bad time. She couldn't help hearing the veiled remarks here and there in the village that his temper was none too sweet these days.

She hadn't known it until that moment, that she had been counting on the harvest supper to make things come right between them. It had always been a time of great happiness for her, and for Alain too—the culmination of a year's work. The hectic rush to get the corn harvested. The smell of the newly-reaped fields after the rain had fallen. The simple but sincere service in the old church, and finally the supper. Clock House bedecked with the huge arrangements of the floral art Mrs. Smith was so good at. The bright gleam of dark oak furniture. Megan had always felt close to the land, and suspected she must have come from farming stock from way back. She seemed to understand so much, and had no idea where her knowledge had come from. She had once asked her father about this, but as usual he was enveloped in the book he was working on and answered her with a vague, 'Your mother used to talk of her grandparents, I believe they were of farming stock.'

Megan pulled herself back from her musings. She would not attend the supper. Alain had outlined his feelings by pushing that slip in the letter-box. She would outline hers by not attending.

The following morning on the way to work, it occurred to her that Ray had probably received a backlash himself from Alain. She had been too immersed in her own miseries to think about this, and felt contrite.

'I suppose I got you into trouble again last night,' she said as soon as she saw him. 'I am sorry, I only wanted to thank you.'

'Not to worry,' he said cheerfully. 'I do admit the atmosphere was decidedly chilly after you left. A pity, really, as he'd just handed me an invitation to the harvest supper. I quite expected him to take it back again, but he didn't.'

Megan looked away. So Alain had taken the trouble to invite Ray and snub her. For Iris? she wondered. 'Did you accept?' she asked casually as she took the cover off the typewriter.

'Well,' said Ray thoughtfully, 'I didn't feel I could do anything else. You see, I had a feeling it was a sort of olive branch, and I gather it's rather a special occasion in the village life. It would be quite an experience for a townee like me. So we go.'

'We?' queried Megan, looking up at him quickly.

He grinned. 'We,' he said firmly. 'I don't intend going alone, not with Miss Markham on the loose. Mr. Drew already considers I've pinched one of his girl-friends, and if I repeat the performance my obituary will turn out to be a whodunnit!'

Megan grinned weakly. 'I keep telling you, not girl-friend—sister.'

Another impudent grin greeted this assertion. 'I know,' he agreed, 'but in my opinion, methinks the lady doth protest too much.'

Megan decided not to argue the point—on that, or the assumption that she would accompany him to the harvest supper. She had no intention of attending, and in spite of Ray's comments knew he was quite capable of looking after himself. She also suspected that he was not averse to putting Alain's back up, and it was not surprising considering Alain's antagonistic approach. She had till the end of the week to think up a good excuse for absenting herself.

When Saturday came, however, it was Ray and not Megan who provided the excuse. He had sneezed several times on Friday and complained of a heavy head. Megan was not surprised when he rang her on Saturday morning with a hoarse voice, regretting he would have to bow out of the evening's entertainment. Megan tried not to sound too happy about it, but was not entirely successful.

'Megan, are you smiling?' he croaked. 'You weren't keen on going anyway, were you?'

Megan hastily told him she would pop up later to make sure he was all right, to which he replied that it was very kind of her but Mrs. White was on duty. Also his sister had just rung him, and he had no doubt that she would put in an appearance, if not that evening, the next morning, and if Megan could fight her way past the self-appointed nurses, he would be delighted to see her the next day.

Megan attended the church service that morning, keeping well to the back of the church so that she could be first out and on the way home before Alain left. He always stopped for a chat with the vicar anyway, so Megan knew she had lots of leeway. In some ways she dreaded meeting him. She had done nothing, but she could well imagine the trend of his thoughts. She couldn't bear it if he just ignored her, and she lacked the courage to put it to the test.

The supper began at eight. Once again Megan was grateful for her father's absentmindedness. He never attended anyway, and the fact that Megan hadn't even mentioned the thanksgiving meant that she would receive no surprised queries as to why she was not attending.

At seven-thirty, she had just finished clearing the dinner table and was starting to wash the dishes, when she heard the roar of the sports car. She frowned, but carried on with her task. When she heard the door bell peal, she almost dropped the dish she was wiping. Voices in the hall told her her father had answered the bell. There was a short conversation and the kitchen door swung open. Megan kept her back to it and started to wash the already washed dishes, madly concentrating on the task.

'I know Hallett's excuse. What's yours?' Alain grated out.

Megan studiously placed a plate on the draining board and took her time in answering, simply because she didn't know what to say. Alain was in no mood for flippancy.

'Well?' he persisted. 'And stop washing that damned plate! You must have got down to the pattern by now.'

Megan placed the dish next to the other one and slowly turned to face him. One quick look at his chiselled features and her glance dropped away from him.

'Since when have you been lost for words?' he goaded. Then he exploded, 'By heaven, Hallett's got a lot to answer for! You used to be pretty outspoken. Look at you now, nervous as a kitten.'

Megan's fingers gripped the tea-towel hard.

'Are you changing or coming as you are?' he demanded.

In half-surprise she glanced down at her blouse and trousers, now covered by a wisp of an apron, then she got the message. 'I'm not going anywhere,' she said quietly.

'Why? Because Hallett's confined to bed?' he grated out. 'It's a wonder you're not up there nursing him!'

Megan was terrified her father would hear. 'For goodness' sake keep your voice down,' she said coldly.

Alain's eyes were hard. 'You mean he doesn't know his daughter's making a fool of herself over Hallett?'

'Get out!' Megan shouted at him. Never in her whole life had she ever said a thing like that to Alain, but she was past caring. 'Go back to your guests,' she blazed. 'As you said, I've got a spot of nursing to do.'

A muscle moved at the side of his mouth and he moved swiftly towards her. Before she could move he had whipped the apron away from her, placed his hands round her waist and slung her up over his shoulder.

'Put me down!' she raged. 'I've some gruel to prepare for the invalid.' Her fists pounded his shoulder. He stopped her legs from kicking out by placing an arm tight against them, and apart from her arms, she couldn't move.

'You can help dish out the baked potatoes,' he

ground out between clenched teeth. 'You're not going near Romeo tonight.'

She was still struggling and protesting as he carried her out of the kitchen and through to the hall. Her father came out of the study door, his brows raised. Then he smiled at Alain. 'Have a good time,' he said, and went back to his work.

Vaguely Megan thought she would have to do something about her father. As Alain had said, he wasn't there half the time. She was all but flung into the car, and as she struggled to get out again, Alain warned her in no uncertain terms. 'You can sulk all night,' he rasped, 'but you're attending the supper. Got that?'

The car jerked forward and they were on their way before Megan could answer.

Once there, she found she wasn't even going to be allowed to sulk in peace. In the same fashion that he had carried her out of her house, he carried her into the farmhouse when she obstinately sat in the car refusing to get out. Megan's flushed cheeks and blazing eyes took in the amused looks and outright grins from the villagers as Alain threaded his way past them with his captive.

She would never ever forgive him. This time he had really gone too far. He didn't release her until they reached the kitchen when he put her down with an abrupt, 'Make yourself useful,' and left her to it.

She glared at his retreating back, then turned to find Mrs. Smith's somewhat startled eyes on her.

Iris came in a few minutes later. 'You couldn't, of course, arrive like everybody else, could you?' she said waspishly.

Megan didn't bother to answer, but started to help Mrs. Smith.

'Just as long as she's here, it don't much matter,' commented Mrs. Smith in her blunt way. 'She knows how things are done.'

Megan could have hugged her. It was obvious she did not appreciate Iris's help.

The supper was held in one of the large barns, of ample size to accommodate the amount of villagers who attended. Long trestles were placed running lengthwise across the barn. The top table was reserved for the local dignitaries. Megan normally sat there, next to Alain. She didn't know how this had come about, she suspected it went back a long way, to when Alain thought it advisable to keep an eye on her. She wondered where she would be sitting this time, and had a feeling she would be delegated to the ranks. Well, she didn't mind one bit. The further she sat from Alain the better for all concerned! She had only been roped in because she had always helped.

Coping with that number of people was no easy task, although things were now down to a fine art.

Salad bowls were placed strategically along the tables, together with mounds of freshly-cut slices of french loaves, leaving only the traditional baked potatoes and roast beef to be served. For this one special occasion, wine was served and there was plenty of it, so there was not the problem of serving hot drinks after the meal.

Iris stood watching Megan first test, then take the trays of potatoes out of the large kitchen oven. She wore a deceptively simple shift dress of orange linen. Megan, glancing at her, took in the low neck of the dress, a come-hither sign if there ever was one. She wondered if Alain were impressed. It ought, she thought, keep his mind off other matters, such as her doing the disappearing act at the first given opportunity. The use of candles would make this an easy task; there would be plenty of shadows. This again was an old tradition at Clock House. It dated back to the times when there was no such thing as electric light. The original candelabra were brought out for this occasion and placed in the middle of each table, giving just the required amount of light.

Loaded with a heavy tray of the hot potatoes, Megan brushed past Iris, who gave a slight start and anxiously examined her dress, then asked Mrs. Smith if there was an apron she could borrow. Mrs. Smith broke off from her task of cutting slices of roast beef and with a martyred expression provided her with one of her own. As she was a lady of ample proportions, it took Iris quite some time to adjust it to her satisfaction. Mrs. Smith, now back to her task, muttered softly to Megan, 'By the time she gets that right, it will be time to sit down.'

Megan hid a grin and started to collect the plates ready to put the slices of beef on.

'Now,' said Iris importantly, 'what shall I do?'

Considering they were on the last lap, Megan thought Mrs. Smith showed remarkable restraint. 'You can start taking these plates in,' she said. 'Start with the top table.'

Iris picked up one of the trays Megan had put several plates on, and started off. She got as far as the door, then came back again. To Mrs. Smith's disgust and Megan's hastily suppressed amusement, she started to take the overall off. Then, giving her hair a final pat, she sailed out with the tray.

As Megan served the lower tables, she felt Alain's eye on her. He sat in the centre of the top table, Iris beside him. Having served the top table, she evidently considered she had done her part.

She sat where Megan usually sat and Megan was relieved. She spotted an empty seat next to Mr. Tilson and asked him to keep it for her. It was well away from the top table and out of sight of Alain's watching eyes.

When the last plate had been served, and Mrs.

Smith taken her seat, Megan returned her tray to the kitchen. She took her time about returning to the barn, and to her consternation found everyone waiting for her. Alain was standing and she knew he was waiting to say grace. As she prepared to join Mr. Tilson, his deep voice cut across the expanse of the barn. 'Your place is here.'

Megan was forced to walk the length of the barn to the top table. The seat beside Alain was now vacant, and a furious Iris seated a few chairs away from him. As soon as Megan joined him, he said grace and the supper began.

Megan was not happy. She liked to know where she stood. A furious Alain one minute, and an olive branch the next, was a little much for her to swallow. She couldn't fathom what had brought the sudden change about. Had Iris annoyed him too? Was he at last putting his foot down? It was a wonder to Megan that he had stood any nonsense from her at all. While she toyed with her food, she darted a quick glance to where Iris was sitting next to Colonel Lamb's son, who looked only too ready to be entertained, and Iris was evidently making the most of it. Her girlish laugh trilled out several times, and Megan caught her stealing a quick glance under her incredibly long lashes towards Alain, at that precise moment in conversation with Mr. Browne.

So that was it! thought Megan. A lovers' tiff. At

a further trill of laughter, Megan darted a look at Alain. He didn't look much put out, but she knew he was not one to show his feelings—at least, she corrected herself, he hadn't been. She idly pushed the piece of beef around her plate, trying to make it look as if she were enjoying the meal. When Alain spoke, she jumped.

'Lost your appetite too, I see,' he commented.

'I had just eaten,' Megan said indignantly, 'when you persuaded me to come.' There was much emphasis on the 'persuaded'.

To her annoyance he grinned. 'Once upon a time it wouldn't have made any difference,' he said dryly.

Megan knew what he meant. Although there was nothing of her she had been able to equal his appetite in the past. She changed the subject. 'Have you quarrelled with Iris?' she demanded. 'She ought to be sitting here.'

He looked amused again. 'I told you once,' he murmured, 'it's your chair.'

Megan looked warily at him, and thought she could see the reason for his abrupt change of tactics. 'Oh, I see,' she said knowingly.

He sipped his wine and motioned her to drink hers. 'What do you see?' he enquired.

Keeping her voice low, Megan said, 'Tit for tat,' nodding her head solemnly.

'I beg your pardon?' he said.

'Simple,' she returned, 'when you work it out,' positive she had now got the answer. Not only had she been literally dragged there to help out as kitchen hand, but to double up as a useful foil in the jealousy stakes. Hadn't she told Alain that Iris thought she had designs on him? Laughable, yes, but very useful if you wanted to do a little stirring up of your own. 'You're trying to make Iris jealous, aren't you?' she said softly.

Alain's hand holding the glass shook slightly. He gave her a bland look. 'Am I?' he said in half surprise.

Megan threw him a look of exasperation. 'All right, if you don't want to talk about it! I just thought I'd let you know I knew what you were up to. Still,' she said airily, 'as you once said, what you do is no concern of mine.' She was quite pleased to be able to throw that back at him, and sipped her wine contentedly.

'Er—tell me,' requested Alain, 'do I take it you're willing to help in my determined pursuit of my loved one?'

Megan stared at him. 'Help?' she asked, slightly stunned. Alain had never asked her for help, it was usually the other way around. One part of her was elated, for now they were truly friends again, but the other part was sad. She did wish he had chosen a nicer person than Iris. Of course perhaps in time, when all the corners had been knocked off . . .

'Yes, help,' Alain said slowly, his grey eyes meeting her wide ones. 'You could, you know.'

Megan frowned. 'How?' she asked. 'Frankly, I think you've done enough already. She was absolutely furious when you let me pinch her chair.'

'Your chair,' corrected Alain, then stared down into his glass. 'Are you game?' he said abruptly.

Megan grinned. They were back on the old status. The times he'd said that in the past! She couldn't help responding, 'Of course! You'll have to lead the way. I'm not very experienced in these matters, I'm liable to put my foot in it.'

'Right!' Alain grinned back at her. 'Just follow my lead. And don't look surprised at anything I do.'

Megan was already surprised, but nodded her head.

It was as well he had warned her, for the rest of the evening turned out to be a revelation for her. When supper was over, Alain courteously stood behind her chair and moved it away from her when she stood. If she felt he rather overdid the chivalry act she held her tongue, but it was nothing to what followed.

It was the custom for a few selected guests to stay on after the supper and take coffee in Alain's sitting-room. As they walked from the barn to the house, Megan found Alain's arm around her waist. Her first surprised reaction was to jerk away, but the pressure he held her in reminded her of their pact. Iris was forced to follow behind with Mr. Browne, but Megan could feel her eyes on her back and wondered which obituary would be written up first, hers or Ray's.

When they reached the house, Iris pointedly reminded Megan that Mrs. Smith could do with some help in serving the coffee. Alain stepped in smartly by remarking that he thought Megan had done enough already. She was a working girl these days, and entitled to a little relaxation. The 'working girl' bit must have hit Iris, a lady of leisure until she found something befitting her station, and that something, Megan presumed, was marriage to a man in the high income bracket—such as Alain.

When his guests were seated, Alain joined Megan on the settee, sitting close to her, his arm placed along the back, encompassing her within the circle of his arm. Embarrassing as it was, Megan had to go through with it. Iris flounced out of the room, for she was now committed to helping Mrs. Smith herself. Megan felt sorry for Mrs. Smith—in that mood Iris would be more of a liability than a help.

'Perhaps I ought,' she murmured, and began to get up, but Alain's arm came down from the back of the seat and round her waist, pulling her firmly back again.

'You'll stay put, Tuppence,' he chided. 'This is only the start,' and then he joined in a lively discussion developing between the rest of his guests.

Megan was absolutely astounded that no one seemed to think Alain's behaviour towards her odd. It appeared to be taken as a normal happening, and of no especial interest to anybody but Iris. She began to feel slightly apprehensive. Surely Alain had done enough to bring Iris to heel? She must, thought Megan, have given him an awfully bad time to have brought this punishment on her head. At this rate, by the end of the evening she should be ready to fall into his arms, and the wedding date fixed.

After coffee, Mrs. Smith joined the company. All available seating was taken, and Alain beckoned her to join them on the settee, obligingly moving even closer to Megan to make space for her. He still did not relinquish his arm around Megan, and she found she had only to move her head a fraction and it would be resting on his wide shoulder.

At this stage she was quite unable to look in Iris's direction, but knew she was, to all intents and purposes, finding Don Lamb's company fascinating, if the fluted laughs coming from that part of the room were anything to go by. One thing Megan did know for certain; if Alain and Iris did marry, she did not expect to be on the list of accepted guests at Clock House!

A tiny pain caught her heart. It was not physical, but something entirely different. In his determination to win Iris, Alain had not foreseen that, or if he had—he just hadn't cared. Iris was not one to forget an evening like this, and Megan really couldn't blame her.

If she thought Alain had gone far enough, there was worse to follow. Eventually most of the guests drifted away and Mrs. Smith retired, leaving only Megan, Alain and Iris, plus Don Lamb, whom Iris clung to with as much determination as Alain had clamped on Megan.

Megan wanted to go home. She was tired of the game and felt it had gone on long enough. She was even beginning to feel sorry for Iris.

To her horror, Iris suggested a walk before the close of the evening. 'It's such a beautiful night,' she declared, giving Don a provocative glance under her lashes. 'I adore moonlight, don't you?'

As a gentleman, and having spent most of the evening receiving come-hither signs, he was hardly likely to refuse, Megan thought apprehensively as she glanced at Alain, who to her annoyance agreed.

'Good idea. Come on, Tuppence, I'll race you to the old spinney!'

In spite of her keenness to take the night air, Iris lingered on the walk, making certain that Alain and Megan were in the near vicinity; and when Alain stopped to show Megan where he had planted some young firs to replace the Dutch elms lost through disease, she came back to join them. When the sudden cry of a barn owl shrilled out near them, she flung herself into Alain's arms, but Alain proved most ungentlemanly about the whole thing by immediately disengaging himself from her hold and chiding her on her nervousness. 'Surely you know the hoot of an owl by now?' he mocked.

Don, who had gone on ahead in the hope of Iris joining him, now returned to the company and the four resumed the walk.

A slightly desperate Iris now threw all guns into the fray. She caught hold of Don's arm. 'I'm cold,' she said prettily, and obligingly Don placed his arm around her.

'How about you, Tuppence?' asked Alain.

'I'm fine,' said Megan hastily, guessing his intention.

Iris pulled Don's attention to a gnarled old oak they were just passing. 'A witch was supposed to live in that,' she commented, 'there's a large hole the other side of it. Come on, I'll show you, we ought to be able to see it.'

Recognising the tactics, Megan wondered whether Alain would rise to the bait and accompany them, thus refusing to give Iris the opportunity of the quiet little session with Don that she was angling for in order to arouse some jealous response from him. But he strode on ahead regardless. The spinney came into view, and catching Megan's hand Alain ascended the hill, pulling her up with him. When they reached the top, although breathless, Megan had to admit it was worth the effort. She had seen the view many times before, but never in moonlight. The gentle rays washed over the surrounding countryside, catching here and there the graceful silver birches and giving them a magical glow.

She gazed out, lost in wonder, unaware that Alain still held her hand. When he pulled her gently towards him she came to with a start, and giving him an indignant look attempted to pull away from him.

'We should,' he said softly, 'be well outlined up here, don't you think?'

Megan saw the plan. No matter where Iris was, she could not fail to see the two figures silhouetted on the top of the hill. She straightened her lips and allowed herself to be pulled into his arms, whispering fiercely, 'What I do for England! How long do we have to keep this up?' she muttered, gazing up at him.

His answer was the last one she expected. He bent his head and she thought he was going to say something, but instead he kissed her gently, his lips touching hers with feather-lightness.

Megan gasped. 'That,' she said furiously, 'was not cricket! There was no need to go that far. I'm going back, I...'

The sentence hung in mid-air as his lips stifled it. Megan was through with acting and struggled to free herself, but he had the advantage of already having his arms firmly around her. She was forced to accept the kiss, no longer light and certainly not brotherly! Megan had never been kissed like that before. Her heart thudded and her senses swam. She felt as if he were draining her very life blood.

When he lifted his head, she was too weak to move out of the warmth of his arms and he did not attempt to put her away from him. Just held her close. Finding her breath, she said weakly, 'I want to go home, Alain.'

He kissed her forehead. 'Home we go, then,' he murmured.

Megan had forgotten about Iris and Don. She had forgotten everything except the way she felt. On the way back to her home, Alain chatted about this and that, and Megan tried hard to concentrate and quell the thoughts pounding through her brain. She had made an awful discovery. She was in love with Alain! As his kiss had not been brotherly, so her feelings were far from sisterly! She was utterly horrified, for how had it come about? She had often wondered if she would recognise love when it came, but had never thought it would come in such a devastating way, or that the quest would be such a hopeless one.

When they reached her home, she was surprised

when he got out too, and stood gazing down at her. 'Come and help us demolish the rest of the roast beef tomorrow,' he said lightly.

Megan started. Surely he wasn't going to go on with it? Her heart jerked. She couldn't! It was unthinkable. He knew her so well, it would not take him long to spot what had happened, and he would feel awful then, she knew he would.

'No,' she said hastily, 'I can't.'

He stiffened. 'Going to Hallett's?' he said softly yet menacingly. 'Even though I need your help?'

Megan closed her eyes. He was putting her on the rack, although he didn't know it. He was only concerned with his love. She very nearly broke down, but managed to get out, 'I must . . . you don't understand.' She couldn't go on, couldn't tell him that she loved him desperately, and always would.

She heard the indrawn breath. 'You really have gone overboard for him, haven't you?' he said quietly. 'I won't say I admire your choice. You're going to get hurt, Tuppence.' He turned away abruptly. 'Well, have it your way,' he added through clenched teeth, 'just remember that I warned you!'

Megan stood watching the tail lights of the car disappear down the lane through a haze of tears. 'Going to get hurt'. The words echoed around her. As if it hadn't already happened, she thought bitterly.

CHAPTER SEVEN

MEGAN did not go to see Ray the next day. Things were complicated enough, without adding fuel to the fire. In a village that size, not much went on that was unobserved; her visit to The Foxes, for instance, on a weekend, especially as it was probably common knowledge by now that Ray was off colour, would be bound to cause more speculation.

Normally, Megan would not have worried, but life was no longer normal. She had been shaken out of her placid existence with a resounding crash. She sighed as she looked out of the sitting-room window, idly noticing that the lawn wanted cutting—well, that would give her something to do. Above all, she had to keep busy.

Keeping busy was one thing, stopping one's thoughts entirely another, Megan found, as she passed up and down the strip of lawn in front of the house with the mower. She had only to close her eyes to feel again the warmth of Alain's arms. Was he at that moment holding Iris the same way? Her heart jolted when she recalled the way he had kissed her forehead afterwards. His way of saying thank you for playing the part so well? She thought it must have been. It was just the sort of thing a brother would have done to a kid sister he was fond of.

Megan was grateful when Monday came. She hated to think how she would have fared had she not had a job to lose herself in. As she let herself in at The Foxes, she wondered whether Ray had recovered, and was pleased to hear his cheery greeting when he joined her in the office.

'Joanna's here,' he said. 'She'll come and introduce herself later, she's just slipped down to the village for some extra groceries.' He grinned. 'We've decided to do a spot of entertaining, and you're cordially invited to dinner tonight—your father, too, of course.'

For one awful moment Megan wondered whether it was going to be an invitation extended to Alain as well in return for his harvest supper invitation. She visibly blanched. In her present state of mind, she couldn't imagine a more uncomfortable evening. Ray mistook her reaction.

'She won't bite you,' he teased. 'And it's not a big occasion, just the four of us.'

Megan breathed a sigh of relief and accepted, warning Ray that she couldn't answer for her father, but would do her best to persuade him to come.

Remembering Megan's worried look when the invitation was extended, Ray soothed, 'Of course, I'm biased, but I think you'll like Joanna, Megan.'

Ray was right. Megan did take to Joanna, although on first sight she had her doubts. Joanna's dress and looks somewhat daunted Megan. She was a slim, petite dark-haired beauty, somewhere in her early thirties, Megan presumed. Her hair was beautifully coiffured, and her two-piece was no off-the-peg model. The only likeness Megan could find between them was Joanna's dark brown eyes, so like her brother's. As soon as she had introduced herself, and held out her hand smilingly to Megan, Megan found herself relaxing. The smile was so open and friendly. 'Ray's told me a lot about you,' she said.

That evening Megan and her father dined at The Foxes. To her delight, Mr. Shaw accepted the invitation, without his usual comment of 'We'll see,' which meant 'most probably not'.

After dinner, they settled in the beautifully furnished lounge for coffee. Ray and Mr. Shaw soon became immersed in literary matters, leaving Megan and Joanna on their own.

Joanna told Megan about her family. Of her children, now of an age to want to cut loose from the apron strings. 'I'm beginning to feel it now,' she explained, 'especially as John, my husband, has to dodge off abroad every now and again. I'm starting to feel neglected, not to mention lonely. I thought of getting a job of some sort, it wouldn't do to vegetate. I only wish Ray were nearer. I worry about him, whether he's looking after himself, or getting enough to eat. Stupid really, but he's the only brother I have and I'm rather fond of him.'

Megan could well understand these feelings. Her thoughts went out to Alain; she had once felt the same way about him. 'I think you'll find he's being well looked after,' Megan assured her. 'Mrs. White is a nice old body. She makes sure he gets his meals on time, in fact I rather think she spoils him,' she added with a smile.

Joanna answered that smile. 'So I've noticed,' she said, 'in fact I'd say he's been lucky all round, finding you *and* a good domestic help. Tell me, Megan, have you any strings to your bow?'

Megan blinked, not sure she comprehended the question.

Joanna's brows raised. 'Courting,' she prompted.

Megan burst out chuckling, she couldn't help it. She gave Joanna a mischievous look. 'Are you matchmaking?' she demanded.

This produced a peal of laughter from Joanna. 'I can see what Ray means when he says you're fascinating,' she vowed.

Megan looked surprised. 'Fascinating?' she echoed. 'Morbidly or otherwise?'

Joanna started chuckling again. 'That's what I wanted to find out. I couldn't wait to see you. He did mention you a lot in his letters.'

The rest of the evening passed pleasantly. Joanna, having to go back the next day, expressed a hope that they would meet again in the very near future; probably, she said, during the end of September, when her boys were back at boarding school and she had plenty of time on her hands.

While Megan lay waiting for sleep to claim her that night, she thought about the conversation she had had with Joanna, of the casual way she had made enquiries about her love life. Strings to her bow, as she put it.

Megan gulped. She had one string—a string of unbreakable strength. It stretched from her heart to Alain's, only no one must know. She turned over on her side, willing sleep to come, but it evaded her. She then wondered whether Ray was aware of his sister's plans, for Megan was sure she had plans. That she approved of Megan was clearly shown, and also the fact that she hoped her brother would marry again; even the dimmest person would have gleaned Joanna's trend of thought. Megan thanked providence Ray was entirely immune from such machinations. On these thoughts, she fell into a dreamless sleep.

The next morning it was raining when Megan awoke. Usually she took the weather as it came, for the rain was needed just as much as the sun, but somehow that morning it only seemed a further damper of spirits. Halfway to work, she saw the rays of the sun shooting through the rain clouds, and the rainbow appear. And that, she thought miserably, was all she needed, noticing that it swept over the Clock House to the church. Iris, she thought bleakly, would be getting her trousseau ready.

It was a saying in the village that a wedding was due if the arch of the rainbow enclosed the church and Clock House. The superstition only concerned the Drew family, and had proved amazingly correct down through the years. Within six months, the saying foretold. She wondered if Alain had seen it. It would cheer him up, he would know for sure that all would be well, and he would wed his Iris.

Megan mentioned the rainbow to Ray later that morning. She knew he was vastly interested in the village folklore.

'So he'll marry Iris, will he?' he asked curiously.

Megan nodded. 'And live happily ever after,' she said quietly, hoping fervently that this would be the case. She loved him enough to want this much for him.

Ray looked at her quickly. 'I wonder,' he murmured.

'It's never been wrong,' stated Megan. 'You wait and see.'

'Oh, I wasn't querying the old saying,' he said teasingly. 'Shouldn't you be getting your trousseau out too?'

Megan stared at him. She was sure he did not mean to be unkind, but it hurt all the same. She cast around for some explanation, then got it. 'Joanna!' she explained.

'What's Joanna got to do with it?' he asked with raised brows.

Too late Megan realised she had put her foot in it. She recovered swiftly. 'Oh,' she said vaguely, 'she asked if I had any strings to my bow, that's all.' She started to put paper in the machine, indicating that she was about to start work.

'Oh, no, you don't,' said Ray. 'Come on, there's more to it, if I know Joanna.'

Megan grinned, for however much she would have liked to keep a straight face, she couldn't. 'I was trying to spare you,' she admitted. 'But it's only fair to warn you. I could be wrong, you know, but I got the distinct impression that she would like to see you married again.'

Ray attempted a look of solemnity that did not come off, and he grinned. 'My own sister too!' he exclaimed. 'I suppose,' he asked with twinkling eyes, 'it's my turn to spare your blushes by not asking who she has in mind?'

Her laughing eyes met his. 'It would be appreciated,' she agreed.

He threw her a wicked look before he left to start work. 'It might,' he said, 'be worth considering, so you can stop looking so amused, young Megan, or one of these fine days you may get a shock.'

She sat staring at the closed door. She frowned. He was teasing her again. Wasn't he?

A day later, Ray surprised her with, 'You didn't tell me you attended the harvest supper!'

Megan looked away quickly, he sounded so hurt. 'Mrs. White told me,' he said. 'She was saying how nice it was seeing you and Mr. Drew back together again. I gather Iris is out of favour.'

Megan did not want to discuss that particular subject, for obvious reasons. However, she had no choice, as he obviously thought it odd she hadn't mentioned it, and she hadn't counted on Mrs. White passing on the news.

'I take it he's forgiven you,' persisted Ray.

She tried to be casual. 'He doesn't hold grudges,' she answered. 'He asked you to the supper too, didn't he?'

'Yes,' agreed Ray, 'and I've been wondering why ever since.'

'That's because you don't know him,' she said quickly. 'You just got off on the wrong foot with him, that's all.'

'By locking you in the pavilion with me?' he asked with a grin. Then he looked hard at her. 'Why did you change your mind? You didn't want to go, did you?'

Megan sighed; she knew she would have to be careful about the next part. 'Because he collected me,' she said simply.

'Did he now?' murmured Ray. His eyes narrowed. 'I can make a good guess why,' he added with a trace of amusement in his voice.

Megan wished she could find the subject amusing, but it wasn't. Nothing about that evening had been amusing—heartbreaking, yes, not amusing.

'I was wondering when he would buck his ideas up,' he commented in the same bemused tone. 'Rather a pity really, I almost hoped he'd missed the boat.'

For a second Megan was perplexed, then she thought she had it. 'I thought you didn't like Iris,' she said half accusingly, feeling great disappointment, because she hadn't thought Ray would fall for a pretty face too.

He looked at her in surprise. 'Iris?' he asked.

Megan was exasperated. 'Yes, Iris. And you're wrong, Alain hasn't missed the boat, as you put it. He's just teaching her a lesson.'

Ray's eyes widened. 'Is that what he told you? he asked.

'Not in so many words,' Megan said slowly. 'But I could see what he was up to.' With this, she hastily started typing, indicating that she was tired of the subject. For once, Ray took the hint and left her to it.

That evening when Megan got back from exercising Chas, her father told her Alain had called. 'Told him you wouldn't be long,' he informed her, 'but he had to get on. I must say it was nice having him call in again, although,' he looked at Megan under his spectacles, 'I don't think it was entirely altruistic.'

Megan could guess what was coming next. He had had his threatened talk with her father. 'I must say,' he commented mildly, 'it's years since anyone attempted to bully me.'

Megan found herself grinning. She placed an arm around him. 'I hope you stood up to him,' she said. 'He's got a bee in his bonnet about Ray, hasn't he?'

Her father said nothing for a moment or two, then: 'He's very fond of you, Megan.' He nodded his head. 'Understandable, of course,' and he went into a reverie. 'Looked after you since you were knee high,' he mused, then shook his head. 'Afraid I've not been much of a guiding light, have I?' he said sadly.

'Of course you have!' Megan said indignantly, thinking that Alain must have really gone for him to have brought this self-condemnation about. 'I wouldn't have you any other way,' she said firmly. 'The trouble with Alain is, he still thinks of me as a little girl. He just won't see I've grown up.'

There was a twinkle in Mr. Shaw's eyes as he murmured, 'Oh, I wouldn't say that.'

'Well, I would!' stated Megan. 'Because it happens

to be true. Why else would he make such a fuss about my working with Ray?'

'Why else indeed,' commented her father, who appeared to find this somewhat amusing.

Megan eyed him moodily. 'Well, I hope you put his mind at rest. He wouldn't believe me when I told him he was a perfect gentleman and that I was as safe with Ray as I was with him.'

'Oh dear,' muttered her father, changing the subject hastily. 'Well, it will all come right in the end. Come and see the letter and contract I received this morning from the American publishers.'

As Megan prepared the supper that evening her thoughts dwelt on Alain's visit. He hadn't even waited to see her, she thought sadly. Even though she hadn't seen him, she was still in touch with events at Clock House. She knew, for instance, that Iris had been seeing a lot of Don Lamb. They had frequently been seen in the local pub together. Alain, too, used the pub on several occasions during the week. Megan could only think Iris was getting her own back on him by such obvious behaviour.

To think, she sighed, she had gone through all that for nothing! She could at least have been spared that. With a pang, she remembered Alain's invitation to lunch the next day. He had asked for her help and she had not been able to give it. Would Iris be back with him now if she had done as he asked? She closed her eyes. If he asked again, she still wouldn't be able to help him. Yet even though she had refused to help him, he had gone out of his way to try and help her. Her hands clenched into fists and tears dimmed her eyes. Such was the difference between friendship and love.

CHAPTER EIGHT

THE following day, Ray told Megan that he would be away for a few days, fitting in a visit to his publisher and a dinner to which he had been invited as principal guest. 'No need for you to come in,' he said. 'Have a long weekend, we've nothing urgent on hand, things are going along nicely.'

Megan was not too sure she would welcome time on her hands. It would be a little more than a long weekend, four days to be precise. She wondered how she managed to pass the time before she took up full-time work.

Ray had told her he was driving up to London that evening, so when the phone rang at seven, and he was on the other end of the line, she was a little surprised. 'I thought you would have been there by now,' she commented, when he told her he was calling from the local pub.

'I started out once,' he answered dryly, 'but the car packed up on me. Luckily, I hadn't got far. It's not quite so drastic as the big end, but will take a couple of hours to fix. There's no point in going back to The Foxes, so I thought you might take pity on me and come and join me. I hate drinking alone.'

As much as she would have liked to refuse, Megan felt she couldn't. It wasn't that she didn't want to join him, she was very fond of him, and she owed him a lot; it was the location that was bothering her. There was only one local, and the way things had been going lately, chances were Alain would call in, not to mention the risk of running into Iris and Don.

With much misgiving, she told Ray she would be with him directly.

One of her gloomy predictions came true soon after she had entered the lounge of the Toy Soldier. Ray came to meet her and ushered her into a corner seat, and as she sat down her eyes rested on Iris and Don in the opposite corner of the lounge. She was grateful when Ray, handing her a sherry, sat in front of her, partially obscuring their view, but she knew Iris had seen her.

'I could see I was going to get drawn into the eternal triangle,' he said in a low voice, 'I was pounced on as soon as I entered the place. I told them I was expecting company. I don't know what I'd have done if you couldn't make it. Who's the new boy-friend?' he asked. 'Don somebody or other?'

Megan frowned at him. 'You're too curious,' she scolded half banteringly, thinking how smart he looked in his town suit and wishing she had thought to wear something other than the usual sweater and trousers.

Somehow it didn't go with his immaculate dress.

He gave her a grin. 'You mean nosey, don't you? It's my trade,' he explained airily. 'I watch people, for my characters, I mean. I think I'll use him as my next murderer. Looks harmless enough, but a lot goes on beneath the surface.'

Megan had to chuckle; he was incorrigible! 'I should have thought you would have made Alain that,' she murmured.

His brows raised. 'Oh, no. As much as we don't see eye to eye, I wouldn't dream of it. No, he's the detective—the hero if you like; not the dirty deed type at all, worse luck!'

Megan smiled. At least he was true to type there. Out of the corner of her eye she saw Iris rise, none too steadily, and make her way towards them. Megan did not like the look in her eye, and suspected she had had a few more gins than was good for her. Fearing she was about to make a scene, she quickly excused herself and slipped into the powder room. A few minutes later Iris came in.

'Didn't want your boss to hear a few home truths about you, I see,' she grated. 'Well, sneaking in here isn't going to get you out of anything. We're going to have a showdown, you and I.' She flung herself into the only chair and glowered at Megan. 'I don't know how you do it,' she said half wonderingly. 'You look so innocent, too.'

'I beg your pardon?' said Megan.

'Act innocent, too,' Iris went on, swivelling round to face the mirror, then she searched for her lipstick and applied some. 'Trying to make Alain jealous, aren't you? Well, you're wasting your time,' she placed the lipstick back in her bag.

Megan all but gasped. Talk about the pot calling the kettle black! 'What about you?' she demanded. 'You've been seeing a lot of Don Lamb lately, haven't you?'

Iris gave a self-satisfied smirk. 'Oh, Alain understands me,' she said, flicking a hair off her shoulder. 'He knows I like company, and at the moment he's busy, but he knows he can trust me—which,' she flung Megan a glinting look, 'is more than can be said for you. Simply because he's got this stupid thing of looking out for you, you think you're on a good wicket, swinging it for all you're worth.'

'I beg your pardon?' repeated Megan.

'Look, drop the innocent act! Remember me? I've seen you in action, and a fine fool you made of yourself. I suppose it didn't occur to you that Alain only took notice of you because he wanted to make me jealous, did it? So don't get any big ideas. You're still a menace—a liability, as far as he's concerned.'

Megan's fingers itched to slap her face. She really was the end! 'So you weren't jealous, then?' she asked.

'Of course not!' Iris said quickly. 'If it had been anyone else but you, I might have been. There wasn't anyone else handy, so it had to be you. But I'm warning you, don't start hanging around him in the hope of him repeating the performance, because I can assure you he won't. He's already regretting that night.'

Megan's heart thumped. Had he realised how she felt? She couldn't bear that. 'Is he?' she queried, as casually as she could.

Iris clipped her bag shut with a snap. 'Of course I can't break a confidence and tell you what he actually said,' she said smugly.

'Oh, don't mind me,' said Megan with sparkling eyes. 'Feel free, go ahead and enjoy yourself.'

Iris's eyes narrowed. She was furious that her words had not had the desired effect on Megan. 'Very well,' she spat out, 'I'll tell you. Amongst other things, he said he'd get more of a thrill holding a wax dummy!'

Megan's relief was so great that she burst out laughing. 'Well, you've nothing to worry about, have you?' she managed to get out.

Iris was beyond words, and flounced out of the room.

Megan sobered and gazed sadly at her reflection in the mirror. If Iris did but know it she had scored a bull's eye. It was only relief that had made her laugh. relief that Alain had not known how she felt, and that was all that mattered. If you were in love with someone it was only natural that anyone else's arms would be repugnant. Poor Iris, she was so jealous that she couldn't see how much Alain loved her—she should have known by that remark alone. It was a very subdued Megan who rejoined Ray.

He looked relieved to see her, and bought her another sherry. 'Are you all right?' he demanded. 'I was going to give you a few more minutes, then come and find you, Ladies or no Ladies. At least you're in one piece. Did she give you a bad time?'

Megan smiled. 'Sticks and stones . . .' she murmured.

'I'm not sure I ought to leave you in this nest of intrigue,' he said. 'I feel partly responsible for what's happened. Would your father object if you joined me for a few days? I could book you in at the same hotel I'm staying in, and we could do a few shows.'

Megan grinned weakly. 'That would go down well,' she commented, 'after what's already happened.'

Ray made an impatient gesture. 'For goodness' sake! It's the twentieth century! Don't tell me your father sides with Drew in his antiquated views of making me the villain of the piece.'

'Of course he doesn't,' she replied hastily. 'In fact he's more up to date than Alain in that respect. You know,' she said musingly, 'I never thought I would say that of Alain.'

Ray took a drink of his beer before answering. 'But

you won't come anyway. Because of Drew?'

'No. But not for that reason,' Megan answered slowly. 'It's not that I don't appreciate your kindness,' she continued soothingly. 'I've hardly the wardrobe for a London visit, and I wouldn't enjoy it anyway. I'm just a country mouse when all's said and done.'

He eyed her speculatively. 'Why,' he demanded, 'do you call it kindness? Almost as if you felt I were patronising you. I'm not, you know. I wouldn't care a damn what you wore, and I'm sure you know it.'

Megan felt tears spring to her eyes. She put her hand over his. 'Oh, Ray,' she said.

He caught her hand and gave it a squeeze, then grinned. 'I'm not helping, am I? he said gently. 'Well, I won't press the point. Trouble is, young Megan, I'm getting a sight too fond of you, and,' he added meaningly, 'it has nothing to do with Joanna. So I'm giving you fair warning.'

As Megan waved him off later, the depression she had felt hovering about her all evening settled on her. Only too well did she understand Ray's warning. If she had been heartfree, he would have fitted the bill nicely, she thought sadly. He had the same sense of humour and was all one could ask for in a husband.

She tried to imagine life as his wife, and found it utterly inconceivable. Perhaps in time, she told herself, when her heart had got used to the empty ache each time she thought of Alain. She sighed, and started to make her way to Mrs. Jones'. She would begin to wonder whether she was coming for Chas or not that evening, if she didn't get there soon.

Her thoughts reverted to Ray, and she realised with a tiny jerk that he had assumed Alain's role. He felt responsible for her, as Alain had, in fact still did, but Ray was prepared to go as far as marrying her. Megan knew a moment's rebellion. Would she go through life always being someone's responsibility?

What was there about her that brought out this protective instinct? Her height? Well, there was nothing she could do about that. Was she too soft? She opened the bungalow gate. She didn't think so. Hadn't Alain told her she was outspoken, and chided her for being as nervous as a kitten? Perhaps when she was older. For goodness' sake, she thought as she rang the bell, when would she qualify for adult status?

There was an appreciable pause before Mrs. Jones answered. This was unusual; normally she was hovering in the hall so as not to keep Megan waiting. Megan frowned. She knew she was later than usual, but not all that late. Perhaps Mrs. Jones had given her up for that evening and gone to bed early.

Megan felt contrite. She didn't want to disturb her, knowing how slowly she had to move. She bent down to the letter box and called through it. 'It's only me, Mrs. Jones. I'm afraid I'm a bit late, would you like to leave it tonight? I'll take him out first thing in the morning for you.'

Mrs. Jones' wavering voice reached her from her sitting-room. 'I'm just coming, dear.'

A few minutes later she opened the door, and although she turned away almost immediately to call Chas, who had also apparently given Megan up for lost and was snoozing in front of the fire, Megan saw that Mrs. Jones had been crying.

'Is everything all right?' Megan asked softly.

At the gentleness of the voice, Mrs. Jones hastily wiped her eyes, which had started to moisten again. 'So stupid really,' she murmured. 'I'm sorry, dear. I thought you weren't coming, so I indulged in a few tears.' She shook her head hazily. 'No, I didn't mean I was crying because you hadn't come. I didn't think I would be disturbed, if you know what I mean.'

Megan nodded. She did know what she meant. She didn't want to pry, but wondered whether there was anything she could do. 'Just feeling a bit off colour?' she enquired. 'I think a good cry works wonders, you know, I often indulge myself.' Arthritis, Megan knew, was a very painful affliction, and it couldn't always be easy to keep a stiff upper lip.

Mrs. Jones gave her a wan smile, and Megan noted that she hadn't attempted to get Chas's lead. She took it as an indication that she would like her to stay a while and talk to her, and was only too happy to comply. 'I've plenty of time this evening,' she said brightly. 'My boss is off to London and I've been given a few days off, so I'm what you might call a lady of leisure. Shall I get us a cup of tea?'

Mrs. Jones' eyes were suspiciously bright again. and she nodded. It was not the first time Megan had carried out this office, and within a few minutes had the kettle on and the tea things ready. Chas, now aware of her presence, followed her hopefully around the small kitchen. 'Later, boy,' she told him, meeting those entreating brown velvet eyes. She knew the matter was not urgent in that sense, for Chas had the run of the back garden for all his immediate problems.

'It isn't,' said Mrs. Jones, as Megan came in with the tea tray, 'as if I'm not grateful. It's just that it presents so many problems, but I did promise, and I know it's for the best really, but . . .'

Megan handed her a cup of tea. 'You drink that first,' she ordered, 'then start at the beginning. We've plenty of time.'

Giving her a grateful look, Mrs. Jones did as she was told. Then when she was nicely settled back in her chair, she began to explain the cause of her dilemma.

'It's my sister, you see,' she began. 'She lost her husband about three months ago.' She frowned, and pushed a wisp of grey hair back into its bun. 'To be honest, I had hoped she had forgotten her promise when I lost my Albert. We'll set up house together, she said, if I'm left alone too. No sense in running two separate places. She hadn't room for me, you see, before. Her husband suffered from a heart disease for years and slept in the spare room so that he wouldn't be disturbed.' She sighed. 'Well, now she's written and asked me to join her.'

'And you don't want to go?' asked Megan. 'Where does she live?'

Another sigh accompanied her answer. 'London.'

Megan could well understand Mrs. Jones' reluctance to pull up roots from a sleepy little village like Meldham and try to settle down in London. 'Can't you get her to come here?' she asked.

'If only I could,' responded Mrs. Jones. 'There wouldn't be any problem. But I'm afraid it's out of the question. She's very active, you know. Of course, she's years younger than me. Does a lot of charity work, helps with the Red Cross, does a stint at the hospital twice a week. I couldn't very well ask her to give all that up, could I? It's not as if I could offer her much of the same kind of life. She would hate it, and besides, she has so many friends she would have to leave.'

'But you have friends too,' Megan said gently.

Mrs. Jones smiled at her. 'Yes, dear, but to be honest, no special friend, and I can hardly say I'm a great contributor in doing good works, and Barbara is. Besides,' she said quietly, 'I have to face facts. The time will come when I won't be able to get around as much as I do now. Barbara knows that, that's why she wants me where she can keep an eye on me. It will have to come sooner or later, so I might as well be sensible about it.' She sighed and looked at Chas sitting, seeming to drink in every word, with his head cocked on one side. 'It's Chas I'm worried about. You see, I can't possibly take him with me. Barbara has two cats, and she doesn't care for dogs. I've thought and thought, but can't find anyone who hasn't already got a dog, and if they haven't, could afford to keep him, let alone give him the walks he needs. I'm afraid that's why I was so upset, I couldn't face the idea of . . .' She couldn't go on for a moment or two, then gulped and continued, 'I didn't want to worry you with the problem, especially as I know how Mr. Drew feels about him, and he's not been exactly approachable lately. So don't think I expect you to help me out, dear, I quite see your position, but it has helped talking about it.'

Megan decided to forget the remarks about Alain, and the fact that Mrs. Jones had unconsciously linked them together again. Her mind was busy with the latest catastrophe, and it was a catastrophe if she read Mrs. Jones' remarks right, of what would probably have to happen to Chas if a home couldn't be found for him. 'No,' she said abruptly. 'He couldn't be . . .'

Mrs. Jones patted her arm. 'I'm sure there'll be someone. That's really how I came to have him, you know. You probably won't remember the Thorntons. Bought him as a Christmas present for their children; same old story, of course, they found out that puppies grew up. I saved him then, and someone else will do the same, I'm sure.'

As Megan walked Chas round the recreation field, she wished she could echo Mrs. Jones' words that someone would turn up. Who would take on a dog that size? As Mrs. Jones had said, the problem was twofold, the feeding and the walking. If only . . .

She shook her head; the idea simply wasn't feasible, her father couldn't help the fact that he had an allergy to fur. Megan would have loved an animal of some sort, dog or cat, but it had been out of the question. She thought of Ray, and quickly dismissed that idea as well. If he'd wanted a dog he would have had one. She knew he often worked in the evenings, he wouldn't want the responsibility of taking him out each evening. Even if Megan offered to do it for him, there would still be the problem of what to do with him should he decide to dash up to town as he had just done.

Joanna? Her expression brightened for a second, then clouded over again. She had spoken of getting a job, not to mention visiting her brother more often, so it was no go there either. Of Alain, or even asking his help, the thought was instantly dismissed. As Mrs. Jones had so aptly put it, he was unapproachable these days, and she wouldn't ask him anyway, not as things were.

'Don't you worry, Chas,' she assured him as he bounded up full of the joys of spring to join her once again. 'We'll find someone, I know we will!'

CHAPTER NINE

MEGAN paid a visit to the vet the next day. If anyone would know who was likely to take Chas, he would. She drew a blank, and was given the depressing news that he was searching for a home for a young labrador at that precise time and there had been no takers so far.

Later that day, Mrs. Jones told her that there wasn't any immediate rush. 'I've only just put the bungalow on the market,' she said, 'and these things take time. Old Mr. Cameron spent months trying to sell his last year. If things get desperate we can always advertise, although I'm not keen on that. You never know what kind of people they are, whether they're suitable or not.'

Megan heartily endorsed these sentiments. She, too, would like to know where Chas was going.

Time, however, she discovered, was something they did not have, as an agitated Mrs. Jones unhappily pointed out the following morning. 'I wouldn't have thought it possible,' she said. 'Normally these things take months. I've just sold the bungalow to a couple who called this morning. They decided on the spot.

What's more, they offered cash,' she wailed, 'so there's no hold-up. They want to move in on the twelfth, and that only gives us nine days. It wasn't,' she said miserably, 'as if I could ask for time to check their credentials, they're friends of Mr. Browne.'

Megan's heart sank. Finding a home for Chas was hard enough, without having a time limit tagged on it. 'Couldn't you have asked for a couple of weeks? I mean, surely they can't expect you to get things settled in that time.'

'I did try,' she answered, 'but they have to leave their home on that date. It's a vicious circle, the people who bought their property insisted on that date. I couldn't very well ask them to put up at some hotel, especially when they know I have somewhere else to go, and I'm afraid the price was a very good one. I hate to sound mercenary, but you know these days every little bit counts.' She sighed. 'I suppose we must put an advertisement in the paper.'

'No,' said Megan. 'Not yet. I've just had an idea. I don't know why it didn't occur to me before, but I've only been considering local people. I know a young couple on a farm in Devon and there's an outside chance they might take him. I can but try, anyway.' She thought for a moment or so. 'I might have to borrow Chas for a couple of days, if that's all right. I'll pop down for the weekend and take it from there.'

As she hurried home, Megan thought of Mary and Kevin. They would be absolutely ideal, she couldn't think why she hadn't thought of them before; but she must not count on it. As she had told Mrs. Jones, it was worth a try.

Mary Gardner, now Granger, having married a farmer from her home town, Tiverton, had been a good friend to Megan in her earlier years. Her summer visits to her aunt in Meldham had brought them together, although her visits were too few and far between for Megan's liking, as Mary only visited her aunt during her school holidays for a couple of weeks. Megan had gone to Tiverton for her wedding three years ago.

She felt a pang at the thought; Alain had driven her down there, having been invited himself. She had been sixteen then, and Mary eighteen. The girls had had one thing in common at that time, a domineering aunt! And they would often compare notes. Megan had suspected that Mary also had a soft spot for Alain, a crush it would have been called in those days, and she wondered if that had been the original reason Mary had tagged on to her at the start of their friendship. But as time went by, the girls really became firm friends.

When she got home, Megan rang Mary. 'Can you put me up for a night?' she asked, after the usual enquiries after everyone's health.

'Of course we can!' Mary said indignantly. 'It's about time you paid us a visit. Do you know Ian's two now? It's odd, really, you ringing like this, we were only talking about you a week or so ago. Can't you make it a week?'

Megan carefully explained that she was now a working girl, and she would tell her all about it when she saw her the next day. Putting the phone down a little while later, she gave a sigh of relief. 'So far, so good,' she muttered. 'It's up to Chas now.'

Having related the story of Chas's plight to her father the previous day, Megan was a little disconcerted to find he hadn't heard a word, and she need not have bothered. She had suspected his mind was elsewhere; he had a genius for looking interested and concentrating on an entirely different subject. She decided there was no point in ploughing through it again, and just mentioned the fact that she would be going to see Mary the next day and stopping the night.

'Does Alain know?' he asked vaguely, correcting a line of writing.

Megan frowned. 'No. And I don't see why he should know. It's nothing to do with him. He wouldn't help anyway, and things are getting desperate.'

The next morning she collected Chas, together with his rug and tins of dog food, plus bowl for the use of. He looked a bit disappointed when he found himself ushered into the car. Waving goodbye to Mrs. Jones, Megan hoped Chas would be a good traveller, especially as, after the first few miles, he leapt from the back seat to the front passenger seat and sat up, looking out and admiring the view.

On the way down, Megan gave him a lecture on how to conduct himself. 'You must be on your best behaviour,' she told him. 'No knocking people down, especially little Ian. Do you hear, Chas?'

She was half-way there when the thought struck her, making her slow up and seriously consider retreat. Sheep! Heavens above! She was certain Chas had never seen them. She went cold as her mind's eye sketched a picture of a joyful Chas pounding after them in high glee, and he wouldn't be rounding them up!

She then thought of Kevin, in some ways like Alain, and dependable. Kevin could train him. Alain had said he would make a good dog if taken in hand. She remembered how she had been able to train him to come to heel, and this thought gave her confidence and she settled back again and concentrated on the last lap of the journey.

It was close on lunch time when she arrived at Nappers End. The farm lay two miles out of the village, and soon Megan was drawing up in front of the old stone farmhouse. Getting out, she was about to let Chas out when, out of the corner of her eye, she caught the shape of a large animal hurtling towards them from the house. She stared at it. It was the largest Alsatian she had ever seen, and from its fluffy fur she gathered it was only just out of the puppy stage. She hastily closed the car door, undecided whether to get back in and join Chas or stand her ground.

'It's all right,' Mary called, emerging from the stone porch. 'He's a big softie, but he will jump up.'

Megan, stroking the huge head, felt utterly deflated. Her journey had been in vain. They wouldn't be needing two large dogs, would they? Perhaps this wasn't theirs? This thought, however, was soon dispelled by Mary.

'His name's Tawny. Isn't he beautiful? I couldn't resist him. You know we lost old Marty six months ago.' She bent forward and hugged Megan, then gave a sudden start and stared at the car. 'Good gracious, what's that?'

Megan turned and met Chas's reproachful eyes, his flat nose even flatter pressed up against the car window—quite a frightening sight if one wasn't prepared for it, and Mary hadn't been.

'That's Chas,' said Megan with a grin. 'He's a big softie too.'

Mary giggled. 'My goodness, he did give me a start. Is he yours?'

Now was the time to tell the truth, Megan knew.

but somehow she couldn't bring herself to do so. The fact that Chas had been the only reason for her much belated visit made her feel ashamed, so she said, 'I wish he were. I'm just minding him for a day or so.'

'Well, let him out, then,' exclaimed Mary. 'You don't expect him to stay there all day, do you?'

Megan wasn't sure how Chas would behave with another dog, but after the initial sniffing session the two raced around at a high rate of knots that slightly alarmed Megan. 'Where's Ian?' she asked, thinking that the poor lad would have to be steady on his feet to withstand the onslaught if he came within striking distance.

'Kevin's got him,' laughed Mary. 'Very brave of him, I thought, but he volunteered, so we can have a bit of a natter in peace. They won't be back until about one-thirty and I've everything ready for lunch. Come on in, I'll fix us a cup of coffee.'

Collecting her overnight case from the car, Megan accompanied her into the house. The house was very old, and low rafters proclaimed its age. Like Alain's, the farm had been in Kevin's family for generations. Children's toys lay scattered in the hall, one small wellington boot was flung in a corner, and a scribbled coloured picture half-finished with crayons, left for use again, lay on the polished dark oak hall table. As she sidestepped a model car, Megan grinned, 'And only one child, too!'

Mary grinned back and attempted to tidy up. 'Trouble is keeping him occupied,' she responded. 'You wouldn't believe what he gets up to. We just caught him taking the cuckoo clock apart the other day. Remember, it used to hang up there?'

Megan remembered. It had been a wedding present and a special favourite of Mary's. 'He got on a chair,' Mary continued. 'It just shows nothing's sacred. As you'll find out one day. How's Alain? I was half expecting him as well.'

'I don't know why you should,' Megan answered half truculently, wondering if it were possible to spend one day without his name cropping up.

'Still coming the heavy brother act?' Mary grinned. 'You know, I can still see the pair of you at our engagement party. Do you remember Ginger Watkins offering to run you round the village on his motor bike? There you were, perched up on the back waiting for him to start up on the promised joyride, and before you could blink an eyelid Alain had you off and was giving Ginger the telling-off of a lifetime. I'd never seen anyone move as fast as he did when he spotted you. And the look on your face! Kevin said he pitied the chap you fell in love with, he'd have to get past Alain first.'

Feeling her heart jerk, Megan didn't know why Mary had had to bring that up at this particular time. She might as well, she thought, get it over with.

'He's courting,' she said airily.

Mary stopped on the way to the kitchen and turned round her brows raised in query. 'Is he now?' she queried. 'Who?'

Megan kept her voice casual. 'Iris Markham. I don't know if you remember her, she only came to the village after you got engaged.'

Mary frowned. 'Not the one who thinks she's Helen of Troy?' she asked, almost in wonderment.

Megan grinned at the description. She nodded. 'I must say it sounds like her.'

Mary came back and stared at Megan. 'For goodness' sake! I thought he'd got a bit more sense. Unless she's changed a lot I can't see her as farmer's wife, even a rich farmer's wife.'

Megan felt sad, and looked it. 'There's no accounting for tastes,' she said.

'Arc you sure?' demanded Mary.

'I'm sure,' Megan said quietly, and to her relief Mary did not pursue the subject.

Kevin joined them for lunch. He strode in with a fat bundle of boy tucked under one arm.

'I know it's asking for trouble,' remarked Mary, dishing up. 'But has he been good?'

Kevin grinned. 'I will ignore that question,' he said, 'on the grounds that it may incriminate him.' He steadied him on his feet, and Ian toddled over to Megan and stood regarding her with his bright blue eyes, so like his father's. The mop of black hair, his mother's contribution, was fluffed up in front. The two gazed solemnly at each other. Megan took in the tiny denims and the carefully patched knees, and the one wellington bootee. 'I know where the other one is,' she commented.

Ian continued to gaze at her as if she were an interesting specimen.

'He's got a thing about shoes,' observed Mary. 'I find them all over the place. I think he's one of the back-to-nature types—let's hope it wears off in time. Now come and sit down, it's ready.'

At that moment Ian spotted Chas, sitting next to Tawny on the kitchen floor, both recovering from their earlier excursions, and made a beeline towards him. 'Oh, no, you don't,' said Kevin. 'I've just scrubbed you up for lunch, my lad,' and he hauled him into his high chair. For a moment or so it looked as if Ian would protest, but Mary hastily placed a plate in front of him and he turned his attention to that instead.

That afternoon Kevin suggested they all went with him to the west field. 'Got a few more bales to pick up,' he said. 'I ought to have finished it this morning, but I hadn't counted on the extra hand.' His look rested on his son, now happily demolishing a plate of jelly.

Mary grinned. 'Now you know what I have to put

up with. How would you like to have him every day?'

Kevin visibly shuddered. 'You're doing a grand job, love, keep it up.'

'Coward!' accused Mary.

The girls spent a lazy afternoon watching Kevin work. The dogs had been left at the farm and put in one of the small paddocks, so Megan had no worry about Chas spotting any sheep. A picnic had been taken and as Mary poured out the tea from the flasks, Megan sat watching Kevin and Ian. Ian, seeing that his mother was otherwise occupied, had wandered over to 'help' his father. He was now attempting to pick up the fork and heave a bale of straw on to the waiting lorry. For a moment Kevin watched him, grinning, then with an expert flick of the wrist he finished the job and swung Ian up on to his shoulder.

Megan looked away quickly. One day Alain would have a son. He would act in just the same way as Kevin had done. She was not one to give way to tears, but she could have wept her heart out at that particular moment in time.

The rest of the time passed pleasantly enough, but Megan still had the worry of Chas's future on her mind as she set off home on the Sunday.

CHAPTER TEN

CHAS was returned to Mrs Jones on Sunday by a subdued Megan. 'I was just six months too late,' she said miserably. Then, seeing Mrs. Jones's downcast look, she said stoutly, 'We're not beaten yet. Something will turn up, you'll see.'

Ray rang her on the Monday morning before she started off to work. 'I won't be back till Wednesday, Megan. I couldn't get out of two more engagements my publisher lined up for me. Joanna's here, by the way; her husband's got some sort of conference on, so I'm detailed to take her to the dinners. Are you all right? I rang yesterday morning, but your father couldn't remember where you'd gone.'

Megan sighed. 'I could have eloped for all he knew,' she said. 'I did tell him I was visiting a friend in Devon, but he was deep in the fells, if you know what I mean. By the way, how much do you charge for an autographed book? I sort of promised my friend one as a peace-offering because I couldn't stay for a week.'

'Considering it's for a good cause,' he replied grandly, 'I shall be delighted to oblige. By the way, the offer's still open for you to join me. With Joanna here we'll be well chaperoned, in case a certain body raised Cain.'

Megan chuckled. 'No, thank you,' she answered.

'What are you doing with yourself?' he asked curiously. 'You appear to be doing a bit of dashing around.'

'Like a scalded hen,' she said. 'I'll tell you about it on Wednesday. Anything you want me to do?'

'Well, you might tell Mrs. White what's happening. I couldn't contact her, she's not on the phone. Tell her I hope to be back by six—and Megan,' he added, 'don't you dare elope!'

Another chuckle from Megan and she hung up.

Megan found Mrs. White watering her potted plants in her small conservatory. She had her coat on and must have been filling in with last-minute jobs before setting off for The Foxes. She gave her the message, then duly admired the plants and started to leave, but Mrs. White was talkative. 'Have they found out where Mr. Drew is?' she asked hopefully.

Megan stared at her uncomprehendingly, her surprise evident.

'Don't you know?' Mrs. White asked, in as much surprise as Megan had shown.

'I've been away for the weekend,' Megan explained.

Mrs. White looked wise. 'Well, I suppose that would be it,' she said mysteriously, nodding to herself. 'Mind you, I'm glad he stood no nonsense from that Iris. Talk of the village it was, Sunday afternoon.'

Megan felt a stab of apprehension. 'What happened?' she asked quickly.

'Well,' began Mrs. White, 'it started in the local. She was there with Don Lamb, you know.'

Megan didn't want to hear any more. Her heart went out to Alain. Why had he to care for someone like Iris? She wanted to stop Mrs. White, but couldn't.

'And Mr. Drew goes in,' she continued, now in full flood, 'just nods to them and gives his order, then stands chatting to Sammy Drake, the barman, you know. Well, this Iris comes and joins him, and Mr. Drew reminds her who she came in with, quite nicely, you know, and says he's no wish to break anything up and he's just leaving anyway. Her ladyship didn't like that, receiving her marching orders like, and says how she can please herself what company she keeps. Poor Mr. Drew, can you imagine it? Sammy said he was furious, still, he keeps his temper and just walks out, leaving her to it. 'Course, by then she'd got her dander well and truly up and follows him out of the pub.' She sighed. 'Some folk haven't the sense to see when they're not wanted. No one knew what she said to him, or what he told her, but she was fit to be tied when she flounces back into the pub. Next thing that happens is that Mr. Drew goes back to Clock

House, packs a bag and takes off into the blue without telling anyone where he's going.'

Megan felt sick. It was worse than anything that had so far happened. She knew only too well how spiteful Iris could be when she put her mind to it. Whatever she had said to him must have hurt dreadfully to make Alain take off in that manner. Mrs. White droned on, but Megan barely heard her.

'Anyone with half an eye could see he wasn't interested. He's got his head screwed on, a more spiteful little besom would be hard to find . . .'

All this time Megan was edging towards the door. She wanted to put her hands over her ears, and in sheer desperation she changed the subject. 'Mrs. White, do you know of anyone likely to take Mrs. Jones's dog? She's joining her sister in London, you know,' she said breathlessly, hurrying on now that she had successfully stemmed the flow. 'He's such a pet, and it would be nice if we got someone local to take him, rather than advertise, that is.'

Mrs. White's mouth fell open, and she made a valiant effort to bring her mind back from the village highlight to a more mundane subject. She frowned. 'That big dog, you mean?'

Megan nodded, vastly relieved that her ruse had served its purpose.

'Well, I don't know. 'Course, my sister's girl lives at Wroxford, not local as you might say, but not more than ten miles away, they've a smallholding. Can't promise, mind you, but I'll have a word with her. As it's a pedigree they might consider it. Always one for a bargain, that Jean is.'

Megan's already lacerated feelings took another plunge into the depths. A bargain, she thought bitterly. Well, that was one place Chas wouldn't be going, not if she had anything to do with it. 'Er... ask them to contact me, will you?' she said hastily. 'If they're interested.'

She didn't really remember getting home. Her mind was so full of Alain that her fingers curled round the steering wheel and she gripped it hard, wishing it were Iris's neck. Alain was proud, he was not likely to seek reconciliation, and it looked as if Iris had got the message at last. She felt the tears spring up behind her eyes. She had had all that, a fine man like Alain at her feet and she'd ruined everything by sheer vanity.

Pulling up in the drive outside the house, Megan did not get out immediately, just sat gazing ahead of her, not seeing anything in particular. What about Alain? For goodness' sake, where was he? If only she could go to him. She closed her eyes. He wouldn't want her. He'd asked for her help, hadn't he, and she'd refused it. A few minutes later she took a deep breath. She would ring Clock House. Mrs. Smith would tell her if there had been any news; she had to do something.

She rang through as soon as she got into the house. Her nervous fingers gripped the cord of the telephone, twisting it round into a tangle as she heard the purring ring at the end of the line. Mrs. Smith answered, and Megan spoke hastily. 'Is Mr. Drew back?' she asked. 'It's Megan here.'

'Just a moment,' Mrs. Smith said, and there was a tiny silence. Megan, suddenly realising what was happening, said hastily, 'I didn't want to worry him, Mrs. Smith, I just wondered . . .'

'Did you?' said Alain sourly.

'Are you all right?' Megan asked anxiously, feeling untold relief flow over her.

'I rather think I ought to be asking that question, don't you?' he answered harshly.

Megan blinked, not understanding—unless he had tried to contact her and she had been away. She thought she had better explain. 'I've been away,' she began.

'Is that supposed to surprise me?' he cut in. 'Because it doesn't. I know where you've been, too,' he continued bitingly. 'I thought you had more pride. I hope your father's proud of you! Why did you come back? *He's* still in London, isn't he? Or did you get your fingers burnt at last?'

Megan swallowed. Now what had she done? He sounded as if he hated her. Because she had let him down over Iris? She gulped again.

'Oh, Alain . . . you don't understand . . .' She couldn't go on, a sob caught at the back of her throat.

'I understand all right,' he ground out. 'Heaven knows I tried to warn you. Well, it's done now. If you know what's good for you, you'll stay out of my sight!'

The phone was slammed down with a force that made Megan jump, and she stood blinking the tears back and staring at her receiver, his words rebounding all around her. He had never spoken to her quite like that before. He did hate her! She had so often received a telling-off, but never accompanied by such bitterness. Slowly the words made sense. He actually thought . . . She caught her breath. He thought she had gone to London with Ray, and that wasn't all he thought! Had Iris so poisoned his judgment that he could no longer think straight, and like a wounded bear struck out at the nearest object? She caught her lip in her teeth and made a headlong rush to her room.

Two days passed, and the news filtered through the village that Iris had got engaged to Don Lamb. When Megan heard the news her thoughts flew to Alain. Would he now make a move to get Iris back? Was that what it really was in aid of? Don worked in his uncle's estate office and was probably earning good money with the chance of inheriting the business one day, but even so, he was nowhere near Alain's income bracket. Megan did not think Iris had fallen for Don; money and position headed the top of her shopping list, and she had wanted Alain.

She felt sorry for Don, certain he was being used as a pawn by Iris to gain her real objective. Would Alain lower his pride and snatch the woman he wanted? The Alain she had once known would have done so. He would have brooked no interference, especially when the woman concerned had shown she was agreeable to such happenings.

Apart from the misery of worrying about Alain, Megan still had the worry of Chas on her mind. Now there was less than a week to find him a home. When she collected him that evening, she was forced to agree that the time had come for the last plan to be put into action. 'I should be able to get it into Friday's *Echo*,' Mrs. Jones said.

Megan then told her about Mrs. White's niece. 'To be honest, I didn't quite like the sound of her, but you never know.'

Mrs. Jones frowned. 'I think I know who she means. They have a place in Wroxford. They buy and sell things, I think.' She shook her head. 'I don't think so, dear, do you? I've a feeling he would soon be up for sale.' She looked quickly at Megan. 'I've been thinking,' she said quietly. 'He might be better off, you know, if we . . .'

Megan started. 'No!' she said quickly. 'It's unthinkable. Please don't do anything yet. Mr. Hallett's back tomorrow. He might know of someone, and he did take to Chas, you know.'

Mrs. Jones brightened. 'If only he could help!' she breathed. 'Oh, that reminds me. Did you see his photograph in the daily paper? I meant to show it to you in case you missed it, but worrying about Chas put it out of my mind.' She limped slowly over to a table and picked up a paper, then rustled through it to find what she wanted. 'There,' she said. 'Doesn't he look distinguished? He was at some dinner at the Savoy.'

Megan obligingly looked. There was Ray, with the usual smile amounting to a grin, shaking hands with a portly-looking man. Beside him stood Joanna, resplendent in an off-the-shoulder evening gown. The photograph didn't really do her justice, Megan thought, it was like those society photographs, with no trace of personality shown.

'She's lovely too, isn't she?' Mrs. Jones said. 'I expect he meets a lot of women like that.'

'She is lovely,' agreed Megan. 'I was just thinking the photo didn't do her justice, it makes her look cold somehow, and she's a sweet person.'

'You know her, then?' queried Mrs. Jones.

'His sister,' Megan replied.

'Oh, isn't that nice!' enthused Mrs. Jones. 'I expect she's awfully proud of him, don't you?'

Megan assured her she was.

At lunch time the next day, Megan had a visitor, or rather two visitors, if a small boy of about nine could be so called. On answering the door she found a woman standing on the doorstep, one hand holding on to the collar of a small boy who put her in mind of the 'William' books she used to read in her youth, and examining the old copper lamp hanging on the porch wall with the other.

Megan hardly needed to ask their identity. 'Aunty said you'd be the person to see about the dog. Er . . . free, I understand,' the woman said. She yanked the collar of the squirming boy. 'Loves animals, don't you, Jack?' she threatened him, sensing Megan's reluctance to answer.

''Course I do,' answered Jack. 'Can I go and play now?'

'Er—won't you come in?' Megan invited politely, feeling dreadful. They had obviously come by bus and it was no mean journey, all for nothing, for she was more determined than ever not to let Chas loose in that menagerie.

The woman nodded affably and adjusted her loosely-wrapped coat, then pushed the boy in front of her. 'I want you where I can keep me eyes on you,' she said. 'Now don't touch anything, and follow the lady.'

Megan led them through to the sitting-room, thankful for the fact that her father would not appear unless called. Then, seating the woman, she started to explain. 'I shall have to take your name and address. You see, someone else is interested,' she lied, 'and it's a case of first come first served, if you see what I mean . . .' she broke off, having spotted out of the corner of her eye the boy wandering about picking things up and examining them, then replacing them, and going on with his inspection. She carried on, 'I'm terribly sorry you've had the journey for nothing, if I'd known you were interested . . .' she stopped, finding concentration hard as Jack was now holding an extremely delicate porcelain figure in his grubby hands. She couldn't bear the suspense. 'Er—perhaps your son would be happier in the garden?'

She closed her eyes at the sudden bawl of, 'I warned you to keep your hands to yourself, didn't I? Just wait till I gets you home!'

Opening the french windows and seeing the figure safely returned to its niche, Megan invited him to take the air.

'So,' she continued, 'if they decide they don't want him, I'll let you know.' She searched for a piece of paper, then for a pen, and said, 'If you would give me your address?'

The woman was disappointed and looked it. 'Bulldog, wasn't it?' she asked.

'Boxer,' corrected Megan. 'Quite a large one,' she said hopefully, hoping to discourage.

It had the opposite effect. The woman visibly brightened. 'Perhaps they'll find him a bit of a handful. Have to be well off to keep a dog like that, wouldn't you? Good pedigree, too, I'll bet.'

Megan realised she was already pricing Chas for the resale. She handed the paper and pen to the woman, and idly looked out of the window while she waited for her to supply her address. Suddenly she started. Really, for a boy who loved animals the child was behaving in an extremely odd manner. She watched as he carefully selected stones to throw at the blackbird perched on the stone wall facing him. Megan hoped he was a rotten shot.

Five minutes later she thankfully ushered them off the premises, and sank down exhausted on the nearest chair.

At the dinner table that evening, Megan watched her father as he contentedly ate his meal, and asked a few desultory questions, not really concentrating on the answers, and thought how lucky he was. He lived in a world of his own. Some people might think it selfish, but when it came to the crunch he would emerge long enough to offer help. At least his way of life was a surety against heartaches. Yet he had not escaped unscathed. The loss of his wife after what was only a comparatively short time after their marriage had hit him hard. Megan frowned. Was that why he had shut himself away as he had? There had been no one else for him. She swallowed. Would Alain do the same? The thought was too painful to dwell on, and she turned to her other problem. Ray would be back by now. She would go and see him when she had cleared the dinner things. He was the last ditch, and if he couldn't help...

Ray was delighted to see her. 'I must go away more often,' he teased after he had let her in. 'Mrs. White surpassed herself in the cuisine line, and now you've come to join me in an after-dinner drink. No, I insist,' he murmured, ushering her into the lounge.

'Oh, dear,' said Megan, accepting the sherry he gave her. 'You make me feel awful. I'm on the scrounge.'

'Well, scrounge away,' he said, smiling. 'What's the problem?'

Megan launched into the sad tale of Chas. Of her dash down to Devon and its result, of her father's allergy, of her not so delightful visitors that very afternoon, in fact everything. Then she sat looking hopefully at him. 'I don't suppose it's remotely possible you can suggest anyone? I do understand it wouldn't be convenient for you to have him, but if you did know of someone...' She sighed. 'There's so little time left.'

Ray indicated a chair for her, and sat down himself when she was seated. He gave a wry grin. 'I'm a drop-out, remember, from past society, and have no wish to renew old acquaintances. As a last-ditch help I'm afraid I'm not going to be of much use.'

She felt contrite. She ought not to have bothered him. 'Not to worry,' she said lightly. 'As I've said on countless occasions to Mrs. Jones, something will turn up, only,' she added sadly, 'it never does.'

'I only wish I could help, but short of offering to take him myself, which is just not convenient, I can't see a solution. How long have you got?' he asked.

'Five days,' said Megan with a sigh. 'Trouble is we can't very well advertise now; if we do, the Wroxford clan are bound to spot it. There can't be two boxers needing homes in this vicinity.' Then, seeing Ray frown, she pulled herself together. It wasn't his fault he couldn't help, and she changed the subject by asking how his London trip had gone.

CHAPTER ELEVEN

IT was back to work on Thursday and Friday for Megan. At the weekend, she helped Mrs. Jones with the packing. Her sister had arranged everything at her end, and the removal van was due to call on Monday and a car had been hired to convey Mrs. Jones to her destination.

By Sunday at tea-time everything was packed, apart from items in use until the last moment; Megan had arranged to have Monday morning off so that she could assist with the last-minute packing. The subject of Chas was studiously avoided by both of them, although it was never far from their minds, especially as he followed them from room to room, his naturally furrowed brow even more furrowed as he tried to work out the implications of the strange goings-on.

Only once did Mrs. Jones attempt to bring the subject up and Megan interrupted, 'Don't worry, he'll be with me. I'll let you know where he goes.'

This sufficed for a while, but when Megan was about to leave her on Sunday evening, she suddenly said, 'I have no right to leave you with the problem of Chas—you've done more than your share, dear, and it's my responsibility. I want you to promise me something. If you still haven't found a home for him in a week's time you'll take him to Mr. Lumby. They say it's quite painless, you know,' her eyes moistened. 'I'm a dreadful coward, I should have gone ahead with it before now. Perhaps Mr. Drew will see to it for you.'

Megan said nothing. Things were bad enough without bringing Alain into it. Part of her knew that what Mrs. Jones said made sense. If only she hadn't mentioned Chas to Mrs. White! And if it hadn't been for Alain she would not have done so.

The next day she waved a tearful Mrs. Jones off and with Chas by her side, drove out to a boarding kennels five miles from the village. It was arranged that Megan would visit each evening and take him for his daily run, so he would not feel abandoned. At the same time she had a word with the kennel owner, as it was just possible she could help, but she heard the same story as the vet had told. This time it was a poodle that had been left in the kennels and a home was being sought for it. 'Not the first time it has happened,' the woman said. 'I suppose it's better than turning it loose, but it lands me with a loss, not only for the weeks of board not paid for, but the continued feeding.' She gave Megan a quick look and Megan could guess what was going through her mind.

'I don't intend to abandon Chas,' she said quickly. 'I'm not going anywhere, and I shall be up each evening to exercise him.'

When Ray heard Chas was in kennels, he offered to pay the boarding fees. 'Least I can do,' he said, but Megan wouldn't hear of it.

'It's only for a week,' she said, refusing to think about what was going to happen after that if something didn't come up. She had promised Mrs. Jones, and she wouldn't go back on her promise. The boarding fees were more than Megan had thought they would be, but Chas was a big dog and the price of everything had gone up.

Two days later, as she drove back from her visit to the kennels, she noticed several cars parked outside the Toy Soldier, and realised with a start that a shoot had begun. Special friends of Alain were put up at Clock House, and the rest found either private lodgings or put up at the local. She remembered previous shoots. It had been her job to go with Alain and charge his guns; she swallowed and wondered who would be doing the work this time. Not Iris, apparently. Apart from the engagement news, nothing much had been heard of her, but Megan was out of touch these days, what with working and spending her evenings walking Chas. It was now almost a fortnight since she had spoken to Alain, and even longer since the harvest supper.

As soon as she got in, she was greeted with the news that Alain had called. Her heart missed a beat. 'He mentioned something about a case of cleaning equipment for his gun, he thinks you've got it,' her father told her. 'He's calling back later.'

Megan knew sharp disappointment. A hope that he had regretted his harsh words was firmly squashed. She felt anger sear through her. If he called, she wouldn't see him. She had enough to worry about without having to put up with an aloof Alain. It wasn't her fault he had fallen in love with Iris, why should she take the backlash? Look what he had accused her of! She was surprised he had even bothered to call himself. Why hadn't he sent one of his employees for it?

'How long ago did he call?' she asked.

'Not long before you came,' her father answered, then gave her a hesitant look over the top of his spectacles. Megan knew what was coming; she was behind with his work, she knew. 'I'll get straight on with it,' she promised, sparing him the necessity of asking.

Mr. Shaw still lingered. 'You're not doing too much, are you?' he questioned. 'You seem to be doing a lot of dashing around lately.'

Megan felt surprise. Her father usually retired straight after dinner to his study, and only then would

Megan start out to the kennels. She explained about Chas.

'Well, as long as everything's all right,' he murmured before he disappeared again.

Everything was anything but all right, she thought miserably as she started on the latest chapter, but there was nothing her father could do about it, so there was no point in disillusioning him. Remembering the cleaning equipment, she hurriedly searched it out and took the case down to the hall, and put it on the table where Alain couldn't fail to see it.

A short while later she heard the door-bell peal. If it was Alain, she knew, he wouldn't wait for it to be answered but walk in as he always did. She heard the door open and waited for it to close again; he couldn't miss seeing the case. She jumped when the tap came on her door and looked up to find him standing there.

Again she felt that flash of annoyance. Had she no privacy? She bent to her work as she felt his eyes probe her face. 'I don't think I have anything more of yours, have I?' she said coldly. 'I left the case on the hall table, didn't you see it?'

He didn't answer, but his eyes narrowed at her tone of voice. 'Ashamed to face me?' he enquired silkily.

Megan gasped. Why couldn't he pick on someone else? Why did it always have to be her?

'Enjoy your weekend?' he added in that same hateful voice.

Megan's eyes widened in shock. He was determined to rile her. She hadn't much to lose, had she? Her reputation was already in shreds. 'Marvellous,' she said between clenched teeth, then shot him a glinting look under her lashes. 'It's not very gentlemanly of you to remark on it, you know. Now, if you would please excuse me, I have Father's work to get on with, perhaps we could talk some other time.' She knew she had thrown away all chance of denying his unspoken accusations, but she was through with the velvet glove treatment. She watched his lips tighten and bent hastily down to her work again. She was not really surprised to find herself yanked out of her chair and held suspended in air before him.

'Behind with your work, are you? That's what comes of burning both ends of the candle,' he said softly, 'and don't address me as if I were one of your boy-friends, unless you want me to start acting as one.'

Megan couldn't imagine anything worse. She had managed to keep the truth from him so far, but her defences were flimsy. Even now she could feel the warmth of his hands round her slight waist. Her heartbeat increased alarmingly. 'Put me down, Alain Drew!' she commanded. 'Boy-friend indeed!'

She hoped her voice sounded scornful. Apparently it did, only serving to bring about the opposite effect to what she had hoped for. She found herself put down slowly, but not released. Instead his arms closed around her and she was held suffocatingly close. 'Not good enough for you, eh?' he said softly. 'My, but you're flying high these days, aren't you? Out every night. Of course you have a key, haven't you?'

Megan couldn't help herself. She pushed him away and had slapped his face before she had time to think. He caught at her shoulders and pulled her into his arms again with a force that stunned her. 'As you're a little past the tanning stage,' he murmured, 'this will have to suffice,' and before she had recovered, kissed her. It was a brutal kiss, and it hurt, it hurt deep down inside her, for he had kissed her before, but not like this. She felt cheap, as he had meant her to feel. When he finally let her go, he was breathing hard. 'Now you know what I think of you,' he said harshly.

There had been no need to rub it in, he had made his point only too well. Megan was utterly shaken, but her misery made her fight back. 'Don't you ever,' she got out in a voice that shook, 'touch me again.' She swallowed, furiously blinking back the tears that threatened to blind her. 'I know you've been hurt,' she got out, and a tiny sob escaped, 'and you're just taking it out on me. Did it ever occur to you that I've been hurt too? . . . And as if I hadn't enough to worry about, you . . . you,' she swallowed again, 'someone who might once have helped me . . .' She hiccoughed, unable to go on.

If he had even attempted to apologise, Megan would have been lost, but his face had a closed look. Her distress had not apparently touched him. 'Beginning to learn, are you?' he said hatefully. 'As you said, once you might have asked for help, and once I might have obliged.' On these hard words, he turned on his heel and left her.

The next day didn't really register for Megan. Ray put up with her unusual quietness and strained features until the latter part of the day, then demanded to know what was wrong.

'If it's that dog that's worrying you, I'll personally take it up to London and hawk it in the streets,' he said.

Megan had been miles away in her bleak world. She blinked and attempted to bring her thoughts back to the subject on hand.

'So it's not the dog,' he pondered. 'Want to tell me about it?'

Megan gulped, but shook her head. 'Don't mind me, Ray, I'm just a bit low, that's all. I'll get over it.'

He walked to the window and stood looking out. 'You know,' he said musingly, 'coming here has been an education. You read of village life and close-knit communities, but you don't really understand, or believe in them, you have to experience them.'

She sensed his meaning, and had a vague awareness of what was on his mind. 'They're just like a big family, you mean?' she said quietly. 'Well, in a way they are. They live side by side from childhood to old age, and there isn't much they don't know about each other.' Except, she thought bitterly, where she and Alain were concerned. Alain had not known her at all.

'Megan, will you marry me?' The question came out quietly, all the more astounding because of its lack of pomposity.

She stared at him, her wide grey eyes holding a hint of sadness in them. Then her sense of balance took over. She smiled, and this time her eyes echoed the smile. He watched her closely. 'Well, at least that got some response,' he said, answering her smile.

Megan felt he had not chosen a very good subject in his effort to shake her out of her lethargy, but said nothing. She didn't have to ask why he had proposed. In a way she had been expecting it. His next words confirmed her thoughts.

'Been giving you a bad time, has he?'

Megan gripped her pen hard. She knew he meant well, but she couldn't discuss it with him.

'None of my business?' he gently teased. Then he

caught her hand that held the pen so tightly, and uncurled her fingers. 'I've a shrewd idea it's very much my business,' he said. 'We were both away that weekend, weren't we?'

'It doesn't matter,' Megan cut in fiercely, 'what petty-minded people think. All they had to do was check a few facts instead of condemning outright.'

'So I was right,' he said softly.

Megan started; too late she realised she had given him the information he wanted.

'What kind of an engagement ring would you like?' he enquired casually.

All Megan's pent-up feelings threatened to burst forth. All this was Alain's fault. His sheer, blind, stupid, protective attitude had even embroiled Ray, making him feel obliged to . . . Somehow she had to get through to him, to make him understand.

'Remember what you said a little while earlier,' she reminded him quietly, holding back her impulse to shout out her feelings, 'about not understanding village life until you experience it? Well, in your case it's so true. I told you about Alain and me, I told you how it was, but you couldn't see it from that angle, and why? Because you didn't belong—you didn't know. You hadn't been around when I was small and big brother looked after me—a habit he's unfortunately never lost. If he had fallen for anyone but Iris, all would have been well, but Iris didn't belong either. Like you, she could only see things from a personal angle. If she had had more sense, none of this wretched business would have taken place. And now you!' she said in exasperation. 'I was so sure you would have had more sense than to be bludgeoned into such a ridiculous situation. It will blow over, you know. We've not been ostracised by the villagers, only Alain has this outdated attitude. Now for goodness' sake let's forget it and do some work!'

Ray's eyes twinkled as he stood surveying her. 'Feel better now?' he asked. 'Having been refused out of hand, as you might say, I shall now go and demand a very strong cup of coffee and proceed to drink myself into a stupor.'

Megan was forced to grin, but relief flowed over her. She had got through to him. He got to the door and turned to face her again. Lightly he murmured, 'You know, Megan, did it ever occur to you that I'm not the type to be bullied into anything—least of all a proposal? You might just think about that.'

Megan's fingers froze on the keys of the typewriter. She had a nasty feeling she was back to square one.

CHAPTER TWELVE

MEGAN'S days were now filled with the deadline. Friday crept nearer and was upon her without a solution being found. There were now only two days left. In her mind's eye she rehearsed what would happen on Saturday. She would take Chas for his last run, then they would return to the village in time to catch Mr. Lumby's evening surgery. She wouldn't shirk it, or ask anyone to do it for her.

She finished the last tape, and sat gazing out of the office window. She had contacted everyone, hadn't she? A range of shots rang out and her eyes drifted towards the old spinney. She saw the small figures of men on the hill, and wondered if Alain was there, and suddenly she sat bolt upright. What a fool she was! Why hadn't she thought of that before! Major Briggs! He trained gun dogs, didn't he? Why couldn't Chas be a gun dog? She would have no difficulty in approaching the Major. He was quite fond of her. He would wonder where she was—he had often teased Alain about swopping loaders, but Alain would have none of it. Her lips twisted; not because he was fond of her, but as he had once said,

'I like to keep an eye on her, she'll be wheedling around you to let her take a shot or two, and she knows better than to ask me.'

She wondered what Alain had told the Major; he was bound to ask after her. That she was a working girl, as he had so diligently told Iris? She shrugged the memory away and went back to the problem in hand of how she could get to see him without running into Alain. Her brow creased for a moment, then she snapped her fingers. 'Got it!' she said out loud.

Ray, coming in at that precise moment, looked at her in surprise. 'Got what?' he asked.

Megan surveyed him with narrowed eyes. She was still thinking. Many of the shoot party ended the evening in the local and often Major Briggs was amongst them; sometimes Alain too, but not often; he didn't have a great deal of time to spare and was usually preparing details for the next day's shoot. It was ideal. All she had to do was go to the local and wait. If not that evening, he would be sure to be there the next. She frowned. She couldn't very well go alone, it would look a bit obvious. She realised Ray was still awaiting enlightenment. 'Would you take me to the pub this evening, Ray?' she asked.

He grinned. 'I refuse to encourage you,' he retorted.

For once Megan did not grin, but shook her head. 'I want to see Major Briggs,' she said. 'He's at the shoot. He trains gun dogs. Don't you see?'

He frowned. 'Not quite, but carry on, I'm bound to catch up some time.'

'Chas!' she said triumphantly.

Ray remained unenlightened. 'Well, go on. I'm only just entering the home straight.'

Megan gave an impatient, 'Oh, look! Chas needs a home, right? Major Briggs trains gun dogs. Now are you with me?'

'You mean,' said Ray, his brow clearing, 'he might take Chas?'

'Of course!' said Megan. 'He's intelligent and trainable and only a year old, he can still learn.'

Ray looked doubtful. 'I shouldn't rely on it,' he said. 'I believe they like them a sight younger than that, but I don't really know. Is that why you want to go to the pub?'

She gave him a pitying look. 'I've not taken to the bottle,' she said. 'Although goodness knows, if this lead peters out, I might well be tempted!'

Ray eyed her sternly. 'Not with me around,' he said. 'Right, we go to the pub. I wouldn't hear of you going alone, not in that mood. Besides,' he grinned, 'Iris might be there.'

'Not to mention Alain,' Megan added darkly. 'That's why I want you with me, as an excuse, I mean, in case he is there. He didn't take to Chas, and he'd be furious to find me worrying one of his guests about him.'

'I'm not quite sure,' Ray murmured, 'that I like the "excuse" part, but I think I shall ignore it.'

This time Megan did grin.

Ray collected her at eight-thirty, giving her ample time to dash to the kennels and return to change. She would not disgrace him this time, she thought, and wore her one and only presentable linen dress of lime green. Ray, in sweater and slacks, took one look at her and raised his brows. 'We must get together some time,' he said in feigned sorrow. 'Perhaps I ought to go back and change.'

'Don't you dare!' said Megan. 'You're fine as you are. The typical English gentleman.'

'Flattery,' he said solemnly, 'will get you anywhere.'

As Megan had thought, the pub was well patronised by the men from the shoot. They stood around the bar in the lounge, the talk mainly of the day's shoot. During this time not many of the locals used the lounge. Preferring to spend their evening in peace and quiet away from the noisy chatter of the shoot party, they would congregate in the public bar.

Megan cast an almost furtive look around to see if Alain were present, and gave a tiny sigh of relief when she saw he was not. Ray seated her in a corner of the lounge, and as she looked up, she saw Major Briggs enter. He spotted her at the same time and immediately made his way towards her.

'So there you are!' he said jovially. 'Missed you,

you know. Alain said something about you getting yourself a job.' He frowned as he looked at her. 'You look different,' he said. 'All grown up.'

Megan smiled. 'It's the dress,' she explained, then introduced Ray to him.

The Major gave him a sharp stare under his bristling white brows. 'In the shoot?' he queried.

'Afraid I don't qualify for the hierarchy,' Ray murmured wickedly.

The Major blinked as if embarrassed. Ray then asked Megan what she would have to drink, and also the Major. Megan felt a spurt of gratitude towards him; he was giving her the time to have a word with the Major about Chas while he collected the drinks.

Major Briggs frowned as he watched Ray go up to the bar. 'Seen his face somewhere, you know,' he commented. 'Got a good memory for faces, not so good on names, though. Hallett? Doesn't ring a bell.' He turned to Megan, his bright blue eyes curious. 'Shouldn't have thought—' he began, but Megan did not let him finish.

'I want your help,' she said.

'Do you, by jove?' he said expectantly.

'Yes,' replied Megan. 'Do you think boxers make good gun dogs?'

His thick white brows lifted at the question. 'Can be,' he said, 'with the right training—why?'

'Well—' began Megan, then stiffened. Alain had just come into the lounge. She watched him glance casually around the room, and she thought he gave a slight start at seeing her with the Major. Someone hailed him from the bar, telling him they had a pint lined up for him, but it looked as if he had made up his mind to join Megan and the Major. Megan wished she could crawl under the table, but then Ray appeared carrying the drinks. Alain stiffened and turned away sharply towards the bar.

Megan started to breathe again and continued. 'I know of a boxer that wants a home. He's only a year old and extremely intelligent—would you take him?' she asked breathlessly.

Once again the Major's brows shot up. He waited until Ray had handed Megan her whisky and ginger and accepted his drink, then muttered, 'Like to help, but retired now, you know. Sold up last year. Matter of fact had a devil of a job placing all the dogs, even so, one or two had to go.' He looked at Megan. 'Boxer, you say? Surely won't be all that hard to place, make a good pet for someone.'

Megan's eyes met Ray's sympathetic ones. The Major didn't know half of it, she thought as she picked up her glass and took a gulp at it. Unaware that he had just sounded Chas's death knell, the Major raised his glass and gave the usual toast. 'Cheers', he said. Megan replied mechanically, then gave Ray a reproachful look; her drink contained more ginger than whisky. He was taking no chances, apparently.

The Major was still curious about Ray, who had not said much up until now. 'Haven't met before, have we?' he said abruptly.

Ray was about to answer, but was saved the necessity by Alain, suddenly standing before them. 'So you haven't met our famous author,' he drawled.

Megan's fingers gripped her drink. She knew that tone—Alain was out to bait Ray. She cast an appealing look at him, but Alain ignored her. The Major looked expectant. 'Meet Vernon Hood, in the flesh,' he went on, 'of whodunnit fame.'

'By jove!' said the Major, standing up and extending his hand. 'Pleasure, sir, quite an addict myself. Trouble is you fellows don't turn them out fast enough. The wife will be furious she missed this,' he said with twinkling eyes, 'great fan of yours. Er . . . tell me . . .'

Ray was well and truly trapped and there was nothing he could do about it. Megan really felt for him. It was all her fault, and for nothing. There was no hope of extricating him, she thought miserably, as the Major launched into reminiscences.

'Damn clever,' he was saying, and Megan could almost feel Ray squirm. To complete her misery Alain sat down next to her. She was furious with him. He had done it deliberately. She picked up her drink and made a point of totally ignoring him, gazing round the lounge, idly watching the groups of men chatting and still going over the day's events. Snatches of conversation could be heard. 'Best day's bag I've ever had . . .'

Megan knew Alain was studying her, but she refused to be intimidated. She was sure she no longer loved him. He was domineering and utterly ruthless; she didn't know why she hadn't seen it before.

The Major droned on; he was now asking Ray when the next book was expected.

'I'm not sure I like the new image,' Alain murmured.

Megan's eyes flashed. He meant the dress, of course. She stared coldly at him, as if he were some new acquaintance getting fresh.

He met that look with narrowed eyes, and deliberately gave her another slow appraisal. Megan wished she could throw something at him. Her fingers curled round her drink and she drank some more of it.

'I see you've moved on from cider,' he drawled. 'What is it?'

From past experience Megan knew there was no point in ignoring the question. 'Whisky,' she snapped, 'and I don't want another.'

'I wasn't going to get you one,' he murmured maddeningly, 'not whisky anyway, perhaps an iced lime?'

'No, thank you!' she bit out, and looked at Ray. With great relief she saw he had finally broken loose. 'If you would excuse me,' he said, 'I have a habit of working at night.' He looked at Megan and held his hand out. 'Megan.'

It was not the action, but the way he carried it out. Inwardly applauding him, she placed her hand in his and got up to leave, but Alain was standing in her way. She saw his fists clench, then he stepped aside. Megan let Ray lead her out still holding her hand. She called 'Goodnight,' to all and sundry.

Once outside, she breathed, 'I'm so sorry, I never dreamed . . .'

Ray squeezed her hand. 'I'm used to it. I don't mind discussing my work, it's flattery I can't take. It's just a job to me. It was unfortunate that the Major couldn't oblige.'

'No,' said Megan miserably, 'and you went through all that for nothing.'

'Oh, I wouldn't say that,' Ray said airily. 'No, I wouldn't say that at all. Some parts I rather enjoyed.'

Megan thought about these words later while she lay waiting for sleep. She had a feeling she knew what he meant. The way he had laid claim to her, just by holding his hand out like that, getting his own back on Alain by that one simple but telling gesture. It was as if a subtle but positive challenge had been thrown out. And Ray was subtle, she realised with a start, also a very clever man. Not the obvious approach for him, like his plots he would have everything all worked out beforehand. To think he had asked her to marry him! Not that he had mentioned it since, but then he wouldn't. A waiting game was more in his line. Megan wasn't sure she liked the position she was in. Was he serious or not? She thumped her pillows. Of course he wasn't! The hand pounding the pillow stopped suddenly. Or was he?

CHAPTER THIRTEEN

THE day Megan was dreading came at last. Saturday dawned and she sat listlessly eating her breakfast, at least she attempted to eat it, but gave up after the first mouthful. Her father looked up from his plate. 'Isn't there a shoot on?' he asked vaguely.

Megan nodded absently.

'Not joining it?' he asked mildly.

Megan shook her head. 'Not this time,' she murmured. Not ever, she thought.

'Oh,' he said, sounding slightly puzzled, but did not pursue the subject, to Megan's relief.

She hastily started clearing up the remains of the meal. She couldn't ever remember feeling quite so miserable and somehow lost. The day, indeed the whole weekend, stretched endlessly ahead. Her life had been so entwined with events at Clock House, with Alain in fact—now she was cut off, she didn't belong any more. She thought of Ray's words about village life. She sighed as she tackled the washing up. One big family—yet she felt ostracised, like the wandering son of a family who returns to find he is no longer part of the family but belongs in name only. He is out of step with them, has missed so much, even in small snatches of news, that he feels a stranger, for he does not know what went before.

She made an effort to stem these miserable musings. A hobby, that was what she wanted. There would be the evenings to fill now, now that Chas . . .

Her father drifted into the kitchen. 'There's a book I would like from the library,' he said, 'if you're not too busy, that is.'

Megan was not too busy, in fact, anything but. She was only too happy to be given something positive to do. The nearest library of any size was in Salisbury, ten miles away, and she would take her time, she decided. She knew from past experience that her father would not be needing the book for a day or two; he never left things to the last minute. She could spend most of the day there if she prepared his lunch before she left.

Salisbury, although a city with a fine cathedral, was still very much a market town. Megan found the book her father wanted, then wandered around the town, mingling with the busy last-minute shoppers. She gazed aimlessly into shop windows, until an empty feeling reminded her that she had had no breakfast and it was close on lunch time. She found a restaurant, but it was crowded with a queue of people waiting for tables. The smell of appetising food failed to arouse any response in her and she made her way out, deciding to make do with some sandwiches. These she ate on a seat by the river, watching the holidaymakers stroll along the banks—lovers hand in hand, children rushing ahead of their parents, and being called back from time to time. A child with a small puppy on a lead, being mercilessly yanked along, hardly being given time to sniff or do what it was obviously being taken out to do. Megan shuddered. Why couldn't people realise that harnesses were the things to use with small puppies? That poor creature's neck muscles would have to be strong to withstand much of that kind of treatment. At least Chas would be spared that.

At the thought of Chas, she lost what appetite she had had, and pushed the rest of the sandwiches back into the wrapping and searched for a waste bin to put them in. She might as well start back. There would be the tea to get, and she would collect Chas earlier this time. They would walk and walk, just wander through the countryside with no special destination in mind—except later . . .

She collected Chas from the kennels, and with a heart as heavy as lead, walked over the heathland surrounding the kennels. She wanted to see him dash ahead as he used to, busy on exploring his surroundings, but he was much more subdued these days. He didn't understand why he had been shut away all day, and was pathetically pleased to see her each evening. He no longer sniffed around in high delight, but kept close to her side as if afraid she would suddenly vanish out of sight.

Eventually they came to a clearing in a small wood, and Megan sat on the trunk of a fallen tree, and Chas sat close beside her.

She stroked his head. 'We're both losers, Chas,' she murmured. 'I guess some of us are born losers.'

Chas growled, and Megan broke off from her philosophic musings. Looking up, she found Alain standing in front of her.

'So this is where you've been hiding yourself, is it?' he said. 'How long have you had that in kennels?'

Megan was too low even to resent him referring to Chas as 'that'. She looked at him, then looked quickly away again. She didn't even bother to answer his question. 'Go away, Alain,' she said quietly. 'You'll probably find it amusing, but it's our last evening together and I'm trying to tell him it won't be painful.'

'Well, I'm damned!' he exploded. 'How long have you had this on your mind?'

She shrugged despondently. At least he hadn't laughed. 'Seems like years,' she said slowly.

'Why didn't you ask me for help?' he demanded.

Her lips twisted wryly. As if she had had the opportunity!

He changed the subject abruptly. 'Why the devil didn't you tell me where you spent that weekend?'

Megan just couldn't see the point of bringing that up at a time like this. 'It's not important,' she said haltingly, desperately wishing he would go away. Soon it would be time for . . .

'Not important,' he said softly yet somehow menacingly. 'You put me through hell and it's *not important*! If it hadn't been for the Major showing me that photograph of Hallett he'd saved to show his wife, I'd still be there. It was taken during that weekend, wasn't it? I also saw the lovely by his side.' His hands clenched into fists. 'Where did you go?' he asked again.

Megan sighed. 'To Devon,' she said slowly. 'To see Mary and Kevin. I thought they might take Chas.'

He groaned. 'Of all the first class idiots!' he said, striking his forehead. 'Well, it's the last time you do anything like that without consulting me, got that?'

Megan knew anger, a cold deep anger. She had been through too much to land herself back under his protection again, if that was what bullying was called. She got up. 'I'm managing very well, thank you, Alain Drew, without your assistance! Go and find someone else to bully.'

He caught her wrist as she attempted to sweep past him. 'And what,' he said softly, 'have you "managed" about that?' He pointed to Chas, standing looking bewilderedly from one to the other of them.

Megan wished he hadn't asked that particular question, not at that particular time. She bit her lip.

'I could,' he commented airily, 'suggest a solution.'

She looked up at him. Her eyes, though wary, also mirrored hope. 'You mean you'll give him a home?' If he said no, she'd hate him for the rest of her life, she thought.

Alain's eyes met hers steadily. 'I might,' he said.

She felt relief flow over her. She wanted to shout for joy, he would take him, she knew he would! 'Oh, Alain,' she breathed, 'thank you! If you like I'll come up and feed him, and exercise him for you, he won't be any trouble, you'll see. Could you take him tonight? And if there's anything you want me to do, you only have to say. . . .' she ended breathlessly.

Alain's hand on her wrist tightened. 'Anything?' he said, and his eyes probed hers.

'Anything,' breathed Megan happily.

'Marry me, then,' he said quietly. 'For that's the only condition I'm taking him on.'

Her eyes widened to their full extent. She stared at him, unable to believe her ears.

He noted the wide eyes and nodded grimly. 'I guessed it would come as a shock, but you'd better get used to the idea. I'm not taking no for an answer.'

Still Megan couldn't take it in. 'You love Iris,' she said slowly, desperately trying to understand this amazing turn of events.

'Whatever I may have felt for Iris, it was certainly not love,' he retorted dryly. 'And that was last summer. I admit to being attracted for a short while, she's very decorative, but that's all. I had the devil's own job in convincing her I'd lost interest.' He pulled her slowly towards him.

'You feel sorry for me,' said Megan, trying to extricate herself, 'because of Ray. That's it, isn't it? Because I said I'd been hurt.'

He wouldn't release her; in fact, he closed his arms tighter around her. 'I'll wring your lovely little neck,' he threatened, 'if you so much as mention his name again. I've missed you more than I thought it was possible to miss anyone. It was always you, although I didn't know it. I couldn't understand why I was so damned miserable when you weren't around. It was like losing my right arm. When I saw Hallett put his arms around you I felt as if someone had stabbed me in the back. I knew then all right! But he'd a head start on me, hadn't he? Somehow I had to make you see me as a lover instead of a brother—not the easiest of tasks when all I wanted to do was hold you and kiss you like this.'

He kissed her gently at first, then his love and need of her reached through and she felt herself swept along on the tide of his love. When she was allowed to surface, she clung to him weakly. A surge of joy ran through her. He did love her. Why hadn't she seen it that night in the spinney? He couldn't have kissed her like that if he hadn't loved her.

'That night in the spinney,' she whispered.

He nodded, his lips on her forehead. 'When you hadn't got the message, I knew it was going to be an uphill fight,' he murmured. She knew he was grinning as he added, 'And you thought Iris was stupid!'

There was a long silence as he demanded her lips again. Then she asked him hesitantly, 'You didn't really think I'd gone away with Ray, did you?'

He held her tighter. 'I was so damned jealous, I'd have believed anything at that time, and Iris knew it.'

'Iris!' Megan breathed.

He nodded. 'There was a little unpleasantness in the local. Her parting shot was that you'd gone to London with Hallett.'

Megan gasped. 'Well, of all the...' she began, then she remembered what had taken place afterwards. 'Where did you go, Alain?' she asked.

He kissed her nose. 'I wasn't thinking straight right then,' he admitted. 'There was only one thing on my mind, to find you and bring you back—apart that was, from murdering Hallett.' He sighed. 'It was a hopeless task, of course. I realised that when my brain started functioning again. I must have been halfway to London by then, so I started back again. I had the sense to realise I wasn't in a fit state to face either of you. Someone would have got hurt. When you phoned you put me out of some of my misery; you see, at that time I thought you had left Hallett, but I hated you for what I thought you had done, because you were mine, and the thought of someone else . . .' He caught her to him fiercely. 'Then,' he said quietly, 'I saw that newspaper photograph. I knew then without a shadow of a doubt that you hadn't gone to London with him. Then I remembered what you said about being hurt, but at the time I was too eaten up with jealousy to work it out. He wasn't likely to take you and keep someone like that in the background.'

Megan decided not to tell him yet that Joanna was Ray's sister. She was very satisfied the way things were going at the moment.

'I hope,' he murmured, 'you've got Hallett out of your system, because I give you fair warning I'm going to be a very jealous husband. I was even jealous of Chas.'

Megan buried her head in his chest. 'Ray was never anything but a friend to me,' she whispered. 'It was always you.'

He pulled her away from his chest and looked at her searchingly. It was all there. Megan's heart turned over. The look of love, and of half-doubt, wanting so much to believe. She must convince him. She smiled tremulously at him. 'The spinney,' she said. 'Oh, my love, you did get through to me. I was so miserable. I knew I loved you, but I thought you wanted Iris and were using me as a decoy—that's why I refused to come to lunch the next day, remember? I was terrified you'd find out the truth.'

He stared at her. 'My stupid treasure, didn't it ever occur to you that it's impossible to love someone and make love to someone else? What kind of a man do you think I am, anyway?' he demanded.

Megan smiled. 'It just wasn't conceivable to me that you could love a plaguey pest,' she said. 'Not with someone like Iris around.'

'Woman!' he groaned, 'do you mean to tell me we've wasted all this time... Come here, plaguey pest.'

He grabbed her. A low growl broke out from Chas and Alain looked over Megan's head at him. 'I shall have to do something about that dog,' he said.

Megan's heart sang as she followed Alain's land-rover back to the village. One thing still slightly puzzled her. How had he known where she was? She had not bothered her father with the information. Her brow creased. She must remember to ask him later.

The first port of call was at her home, to appraise her father of the news. Hand in hand, they went to beard him in his den. His only comment was a mild, 'Well, I thought it was about time—did you get that book for me, Megan?'

After commenting that he would have to do something about her father too, Alain led her out of the house and to her query of, 'Where are we going?' gave her a look that melted her bones. 'The spinney,' he said. 'I can't think of a better place, can you?'

Megan couldn't. It was a beautiful evening. They had just started out when she asked her question. 'How did you know where to find me, and about the kennels?' she asked.

Alain gave her a sombre look. 'Hallett told me,' he said.

Megan stared at him. 'Did he contact you, then?' she asked.

He made a wry grimace. 'No,' he said abruptly, 'I did the contacting.'

Megan started. 'Oh, Alain, you didn't . . .'

'No,' he said, grinning. 'Although when I first got there it was touch and go. I decided to have it out there and then with him—it certainly cleared the air. I regret to say I found myself on the receiving end. I must say my opinion of him has somewhat altered.'

'Why didn't you tell me this before?' Megan demanded. 'I told you he was a good friend. Let's go and tell him right now,' she said eagerly, feeling a rush of warmth for Ray. What a good friend he had turned out to be!

Alain pulled off the road and sat looking at her.

'Tonight,' he murmured, 'is our night. I've a lot of leeway to make up, remember? Secondly, I didn't tell you for one very good reason. I was still not sure how you felt about him, and I'm pretty sure he's more than just fond of you. Any more questions?'

Megan did, however, persuade Alain to make the visit the next day, having utterly convinced him the previous evening that she was not likely to have a change of heart.

The two men faced each other. There was a twinkle in Ray's eye, and soon an answering one in Alain's.

'So you got sorted out at last,' commented Ray. 'When's the wedding? There's a six months' deadline, I understand.'

Megan gasped—she had forgotten the rainbow. Alain grinned. 'There were times when I thought I'd never make it. But it's never been wrong yet.'

Her heart soared. He had seen the rainbow! Her eyes filled with tears as she looked at Ray. 'Oh, Ray! You knew all along, didn't you?'

He gave her his wide grin. 'As Alain has just said, there were times when . . .' He turned to him. 'Man's best friend?' he said.

Alain grinned back and he caught Megan's hand. 'There was no other way,' he said mournfully.

Ray looked from one to the other. 'You know,' he observed, 'I was tempted to try that line myself.'

'Don't mind me,' said Megan indignantly.

'I do so hate,' went on Ray, 'breaking in new secretaries.'

'Sorry about that,' breezed Alain, not sounding a bit sorry, 'this one's got her work cut out. How do you fancy the role of godfather?'

'Alain!' gasped Megan.

He looked at her. 'Got someone else in mind, had you?' he murmured.

Megan blushed. 'I think he'd make a wonderful godfather,' she whispered.

Chas was waiting for them outside the house; they had walked down from Clock House, and Alain had told him to stay when they reached The Foxes. Megan thought it was very clever of him to obey that command. It did occur to her that Alain might have hoped he wouldn't.

As they walked down the drive, Alain's arm went round Megan, pulling her close. Chas tried to work a way in between them. 'Back, sir!' Alain commanded.

'Isn't he clever, darling,' Megan commented. 'He knows who's master—look, he's following behind nicely.'

He threw her a wicked look. 'And that's the way it's going to be,' he said, pulling her nearer. 'Not only with Chas.'

'Yes, darling,' breathed Megan dreamily.